Halfmoon Rising

The Halfmoon Bay
Writers' Workshop Anthology

**Foreword by
A. S. Penne**

**Twin Eagles Publishing
2011**

1

Library and Archives Canada Cataloguing in Publication

Halfmoon rising: the Halfmoon Bay Writers' Workshop anthology / editor, A.S. Penne; authors, Pat Wenger ... [et al.]

ISBN 978-1-896238-12-8

1. Canadian literature (English)--British Columbia--Sunshine Coast. 2. Canadian literature (English)--21st century. I. Penne, A. S. (Anthea S.), Wenger, Pat, 1956-

PS8255.B7H35 2012   C810.8'0971131   C2011-908223-3

TWIN EAGLES PUBLISHING
Box 2031
Sechelt BC
V0N 3A0
pblakey@telus.net
604 885 7503
twineaglespublishing.webs.com

2

Foreword

When I first advertised for others wanting to participate in a writing workshop, I had no idea whether anybody else might be willing to venture out to the wilds of Halfmoon Bay on BC's euphemistically named Sunshine Coast.

That was in the fall of 2001, or so my memory believes, and that first year the workshop had six participants. There were two men in that group, a higher-than-usual male presence. We never did come up with a witty name for our group and so it remains the Halfmoon Bay Writers' Workshop

Ten years on, Paul Blakey suggested putting together an anthology of the present group's work. I have to admit that at first I did not leap at the idea. A few years ago I'd organized a similar book of writings from a secondary school workshop, and fresh in my mind were memories of hours of unpaid work to produce that book! Still, I recognized that the exercise of writing for possible publication – having one's work critiqued as well as edited; rewriting it for more critique and editing; and again; and again; and again, seemingly forever – is good practice for any would-be writer.

Having been on both sides of the fence, as both writer and editor, I know all too well the feeling of being misunderstood by the person on the other side. I know how difficult it is to hand over your heartfelt work to someone who will probably go at it with a knife and fork, burping it out in a completely changed format. And I know how delicate an editor needs to be when trying to nudge a writer towards a more succinct, usually less flowery, version of their work. For both editor and writer, it's all a part of the learning curve, one that is much like childbirth: after the finished product is in hand, the tedium and hair-tearing will be (mostly) forgotten!

The benefit, to the writer and to the world at large, is

that all the work done on the manuscript enlightens each of us a little more. We learn about the precision of language—how to choose our words more carefully (something our politicians could benefit from)—and we learn about finding clarity by polishing those words again and again.

So when is a work of creation 'finished?' Mother Nature would say that actually never happens. But with each change to a manuscript, an author learns something about tightening language, clarifying meaning, choosing what to keep or enhance, and what to ditch or completely rewrite. All of these are skills that are transferable to the larger (i.e. 'real') world.

Unpaid work is the bane of all creators, but especially those who work with words. Unless a written work wins a major prize, the writer's biggest claim to fame is the fact that his/her work is stored on some dusty bookshelf in the bowels of the *National Collection*, part of Canada's attempt to prove we really do have common culture. But even when a book does garner public notice, it's the publisher who makes a real profit from the sales, not the writer. And the editor ... well nobody remembers an editor when a book goes on to win the Pulitzer, now do they? But perhaps that's as it should be, since he/she is really the cleanup person; the one who fixes the smear in the icing before the cake is presented.

What I've enjoyed most about editing this anthology was watching the growth of each piece. Some of the early drafts for the works included here were first presented at our workshop several years ago. Now here they are, honed and polished after hours of (sometimes gruelling) labour, brought to fruition for your enjoyment. This collection is proof that only the most dedicated of writers survive the sweat of the creative process: the hours of rewriting undergone in these pieces deserve recognition and I applaud Flo, Linda, Pat and Frank for their diligence and drive. Kudos to each one of you!

The participants at a writers' workshop generally cover a wide range of writing styles, a fact that is very evident in the pieces included here. But those differences are also the strength of any workshop, the fodder that keeps a gathering of writers functioning at a high level.

As the facilitator of a writers' workshop, I have several jobs. The main one is to provide a safe, unbiased atmosphere in which an author can present his/her work. A second, equally important part of the job, is to enforce the understanding that a workshop is not solely a venue for the presentation of work. Participants at the Halfmoon Bay Writers' Workshop must commit to two equally important aspects of the group: the one of sharing their work and the other of providing feedback to those who are presenting work.

The other part of my job is to remind participants not to try and rewrite someone else's work in a different style than the one used. Finding a way to appreciate an author's particular voice and style is sometimes the toughest part of the critiquing job.

For newcomers, it is frequently difficult to understand that being part of a writers' workshop is not just about being a writer. It's about reading with an understanding of what the author is trying for; about finding the best words to respond to that writing by highlighting what works for the reader; and about an often arduous process of exploring our deeper reactions in order to discover useful and illuminating feedback for the author. As a group, we strive to find careful and judicious comments that won't harm either the author or the responder.

Responders must remain vigilantly aware that the work they are speaking to cannot be judged from their own point of view or perspective. What an author needs is a response from the heart, but also a response that speaks to the intellectual and gut level understanding of the language. So a critiquer is asked to go much deeper, beyond liking or not liking the writing, and to explore how the piece works (or doesn't) for them. To do that, a response often needs to ask questions of the author, questions that elicit what is intended in a certain passage, or what the author had hoped to convey. Because while it may seem straightforward to use words to say what is meant, it's often true that the reader doesn't quite understand—or doesn't understand fully—precisely what a writer feels, thinks, and sees.

By learning how to ask questions of a writer, a participant also learns to read critically. In this way, then, the work of a reader becomes as important as that of the writer. If readers are not comfortable with the style, manner, or voice of the writing in hand, their job is to figure out why they are reacting as they are. If it's a Pulitzer Prize winner they're reading and they're struggling to get through the book, then the question that should come to mind is why (or what) the Pulitzer Prize jury found so rewarding about the work. But also what is it that doesn't work for the reader? Where are the stumbling blocks that make them cringe or reject the work as they read through it?

Each of the pieces in this anthology have undergone the sometimes rigorous process of being workshopped. Over several drafts, usually involving a lively question-and-answer process, we've addressed some of the questions asked above. Through the process, participants have learned that they need to remain open and not jump too readily on any apparent faults in the writing. Because if an author feels overtly criticized, the feedback from others may not be something that she can hear, let alone consider. But if a writer is able to ask questions of readers, it's usually possible to alter those areas causing difficulty for the readers.

An artist creates in the solitude of their studio or home, a place that is (usually, though not always) free of distractions from the job at hand. For writers, as for other artists, the work involves bringing forth something carried within; often something which has been there for many years. The contradiction, of course, is that this work, created by a single soul, is presented to the souls of so many others, others who then respond to it.

At the Halfmoon Bay Writers' Workshop, each author provides a hard copy of their work to the other participants at table. The author then reads the work orally, a practice that provides two levels of feedback: by reading the work out loud, the author can actually hear the rhythm and sense of the language, and the audience hears the piece in the manner the author intends it to be presented. This oral presentation, often the first time an author has heard the way the words work, also allows the writer to judge for herself whether the piece does what she wants.

After the reading, the participants are encouraged to give the author some positive feedback before launching into questions. A suggestion I make regularly is: "Don't just tell the writer you 'like it.' Be specific and find something in the text that supports what you like about it." So a poem about the ocean, for instance, may have a wonderful image of sunlight reflecting on water and the responder will often pull out favourite moments like that, letting the author know how personally she responded to the image.

Then the questions—the real work—begins.

If several of the readers zero in on one particular passage, the author is cued that something is awry. This is where the author will need to learn to remain open: sometimes it's just a matter of shifting a focus or inverting a sequence; other times it's the simple addition of one word. At other times a whole page needs rewriting in order to clarify what's happening, or to build on what's been started but not quite completed.

The feedback a writer hears in a workshop, though— from me or from anyone else—is not necessarily the truth. It's the writer's job, as the creator of the work, to go home and mull over the feedback, see if it speaks to them on any level. Quite often, when I've worked with an editor, the editor has zeroed in on a place where I struggled endlessly with a passage. When that happens, I know—and likely knew from the start—that it's not right; it's not there yet.

One of the best pieces of advice I've ever received came from a professor at UBC's Department of Creative Writing. Keith Maillard once told me, "If you think you've written a particularly beautiful sentence, consider removing it." What he meant was that sometimes we overwrite a piece of prose so badly that it will actually make an educated reader cringe!

Every editor has their own preferences and so it's easy

for me to sing the praises of the writers in this collection. But where this anthology is meaningful, I think, is that all of the writers showcased here have worked hard at their craft. While other participants have come and gone from this workshop, not only have most of the four here been participants for several years now, but all of them have grown with their work, both in terms of their confidence as well as an ability to recognize good writing. Like everything else in life, it's the difficult work that is the most rewarding.

So I applaud the persistence and perseverance of these writers and their unwillingness to give up, even after a workshop where they went home feeling as though all their work had been for nought. Because that's what it takes to be a writer today, and especially in Canada where the small presses are dropping like flies with the advance of the digital age.

Two of the writers included here are working on longer projects. Linda Szabados has flatly denied that her story, *Time and Tide,* is part of a novel, but I have my bets placed on another outcome! Linda is also at work on a longer family history born from the experience of her husband's Hungarian relatives during WW II.

Flo Walker's piece, *Katie Ann*, is a short excerpt from a creative non-fiction work originally written for her family. Characterized by the wonderfully lilting speech typical of Cape Breton Island, this story has been transformed into a mesmerizing manuscript about an earlier era on the other side of Canada.

Pat Wenger is the workshop's 'resident poet' and it's been a joy to celebrate with her as her work is accepted for publication. Some of her latest poems – *Rock Her, Mother and Son*, and *Kite Flyer* – are strong examples of her ability to play with sounds and rhythms as much as the language of poetry. Also a creative nonfiction writer, Pat's prose is equally uplifting and inspiring.

Frank McKenzie is a relative newcomer to the Halfmoon Bay Writers' Workshop, having joined us just this past year. Writing poetry, creative nonfiction and fiction, Frank is as much at home with the dark imagery in a poem like *Unchained* as he is with the lighthearted humour of *Naked in the Mall.*

    I thank all the participants for joining in this project. Thanks for trusting me with your work and thanks for honouring me with the sharing of some of your deepest explorations. Thanks, too, for contributing to a better world, not only through your work, but through some of the most considered and heartfelt discussions on life.

ASPenne
May 26, 2011

CONTENTS

Patricia Wenger

Resides in the exquisite area of Garden Bay on the Sunshine Coast of BC. She is married, an empty-nester whose interests are too many to count. Subsequent to a career in financial services, she now dabbles at her passion for creative writing. Patricia's creative works have been published in *Descant, Just Business People Magazine, Four and Twenty, WorkLifeGroup* and the *North Shore Writer's Association.* In her spare time, she loves to garden, preserve, quilt, and play piano.

Full Moon in San Diego

Turquoise skies have given way to dusk's steel-blue shade as we stroll down San Diego's streets. Although somewhat apathetic, we're seeking a cafe to indulge in dinner. Over time, rest for our weary feet becomes the ever-increasing priority. Inspecting menu after posted menu along the Fifth Avenue strip, we finally settle on an inexpensive pub which also offers outdoor seating. Tables and chairs sprawl along for a stretch outside the building, parallel to the sidewalk yet separately contained by a wrought iron railing. A simple pub, a common street, similar to so many others in downtown San Diego. The air is warm for the first day in January, and welcomed, given we Canadians consider it a novelty (or perhaps even an answered prayer) for the opportunity to prance around in T-shirts and capris at this time of year.

Further scrutinizing the menu at our outdoor table, we each order a glass of beer. The sky now appears to have been washed with twilight and a full moon hangs perfectly in the gap between two taller buildings across the way. It feels good to relax after a full day at the zoo. We sip our beers in silence, mellowing out while witnessing an unfolding street scene of passersby. Some strutting, others sauntering, many are simply meandering, directionless. A steady murmur of voices from evening strollers and outdoor cafe loungers seems to vibrate in the air, resonating much like a heartbeat; like San Diego's own throbbing pulse. This perpetual echo seeps through us, and somewhat hypnotically holds us steady within its grip. Occasionally, laughter tinkling like wind chimes filters through to break the rhythm of the beat. Tourists intermingle with locals fashioning a steady stream of foot traffic, all strolling by like ripples of a brightly coloured river that flows in slow motion.

He passes by casually, like just another droplet carried downstream, when suddenly he stops, dead in his tracks.

Pivoting on one foot, he achieves an about-face and paces a few feet backwards to stand before us.

"You're a great looking couple; I just wanted you to know that."

Wow. How can we not be flattered? But what does he mean? We look content together? Comfortable as a couple? Listen, it can't be our great bodies or designer labels because both are quite obviously absent. My husband Hans is... well, shall we say short for his weight – and silver threads are threatening to overtake the remaining strands of chestnut. (At least he still has a full head of hair, though.) My own hair is flaming red – thanks to some assistance from Lady Clairol. My meno-pot, however, can no longer be discreetly contained or easily camouflaged.

"Thanks," we say in unison. Always the polite Canadian couple. (At least we didn't say "Thanks, eh?")

His guitar is slung over his back, attached by a wide embroidered strap loosely draped across his chest. Black hair is slicked straight back. Sideburns are meticulously groomed into two identical thin slits of black that reach from each earlobe almost to the corners of his mouth. Sleeveless arms permit a view of lush tattoo art which stretches from shoulder to wrist on both arms. Strangely, he somehow presents a perfect walking contradiction between 'grease' and 'polish.' He could quite easily pass as either a male prostitute or an exotic and mysterious foreign prince.

"Because you're such a great looking couple, I'd like to play you a song. Hey, if you like my song and in any way you want to show your appreciation, I'd be happy to oblige you. Hey, you like Johnny Cash?" Tattoo Prince asks.

"No. Sorry." I'm not sure why I apologize. I do not want to offend him though. Hard not to tell we're Canadian now, for sure. (Aren't we always apologizing over nothing? Someone steps on my toes and I'm the one who apologizes for being in their way.) But, in all honesty, the only thing I've ever enjoyed about Johnny Cash was the actor who portrayed him in the movie, Joaquin Phoenix or somebody?

"Hey. No problem. I don't like him either. How about Van Morrison?"

"Yeah, we like Van," nodding our agreement.

"By the way, my name's Frankie. I'm going to play this Van Morrison tune especially for you."

Swinging the instrument around in one fluid motion, suddenly the sound escaping from olive hands strumming this blond guitar envelops us. Music is all we hear as his fingers competently caress his guitar's strings. Frankie's voice, strong, sure, on key, bellows out the words to "Brown Eyed Girl" and we can't restrain ourselves from tapping and swaying in rhythm to his beat.

Frankie winks at me as he croons the words, "You my-y ... brown eyed girl," and I'm not sure why, because my eyes are quite obviously blue. He couldn't possibly be trying to flirt with me? Suddenly, all of those dining outside join in the chorus with him, given his encouragement.

"Sha na na na na na na na na na na shu-agh," smiling, singing, swaying; yet my eyes are gripped by Frankie's face. His teeth, like white pearls, his voice pitch-perfect. Eyes like shiny black nuggets of coal. And I see it. There, in his eyes, between the winks, I see sorrow. I sense the ache, the story. I comprehend the anguish, the longing, the loneliness. A vacancy exists; his eyes remind me to "be kinder than necessary; everyone has a story."

When he finishes with "Brown Eyed Girl" we applaud loudly while the stream of passersby behind him continues to flow. My husband, Hans, rises, steps towards him, shakes his hand in order to deposit a $5 bill. We thank him, tell him how much we enjoyed our song.

Frankie beams beneath the moonlight in San Diego. Stars sprinkling the evening sky now also nod, twinkling their approval.

"Thanks kindly. You're a great couple. Have yourselves a wonderful evening."

He walks away. Frankie falls back into the murmur, into

the pulse that has resumed since his singing stopped. He melts into the river of people that flood the street as the moon shines down upon them. New Year's day. Some are dressed to the nines in sequins or slinky satins. They shimmer in the moonlight, like ripples catching the sun, then they, too, melt away.

The waitress arrives with our meals and another glass of beer. Mesmerized by the hum once again, we plough through our main course with little conversation. Eventually, as we finish our meals and dab at mouths with napkins, Frankie passes us again. At the far end of the pub's sidewalk, he stops once more, dead in his tracks and turns to the couple four tables down, "Hey, you're a great looking couple."

Within moments the sound of a Moody Blues' tune permeates the air like exquisite notes dancing on stardust. The full moon still hangs upon black silky sheets, yet seems to rest right above Frankie's head, like a jewelled crown adorning a prince. Resembling a work of art, or a moonlight sonata, a player named Frankie tenders his symphony beneath magical San Diego skies.

Nature's Heartbeat

in stillness
in silence
in solitude
      I listen
      to rhythms
      revealed

The loon's lament
keeps time
with ocean's waves
like a pulse
infinitely sequential,
splashing upon shore

A lone seagull
cries - in syncopation
against the pace
of a raven's wings
in flight overhead

Leaves rustle
with whispering winds,
murmur
between beats
of falling dewdrops

      my mute pulse
      throbs,
      catches the tempo,
      dances
      to the drum
      of nature's heartbeat...
      anchors my swaying spirit.

Kite Flyer

he stood
a lone figure
solo, at the heart of the sandbar
directing his windswept kite

gracefully, it sashayed up high
twisted and turned with the currents
rose, fell, soared, swooped
      a bright bird
        with strings attached
to a man
alone and grounded
pining for color
aching for wings
and itching
for a wayward wind

Autumn's Air

Shades of grey shroud the surrounding sea and sky as winter's cold, harsh wind bites pink cheeks and pinches fingertips. Like an evil spell, February eats through my flesh as my spirit decays, entombed in its annual mausoleum. Similar to a child who counts days until Christmas, I pout and pine for balmy summer days. Frequently I'm caught ogling maple's barren limbs in March – as if insistent inspection will somehow spurt Spring.

If each season casts a spell upon me, then it is summer that most bewitches me. Like a potion, an intoxicating brew, I'm hopelessly drawn in the same way that the tide effortlessly pulls the moon. When at long last, summer slips into the bay, she's a longed-for lover who sprints to my waiting embrace. From the moment robin's early morning song beckons, we frolic. Or leisurely we linger, passing long, lazy days together. Squirrels scurry about as eagles ride waves in forget-me-not skies. Inquisitive deer timidly nibble offerings of apple, then brazenly graze the bouquet table. A freckled fawn suckles. A graceful doe pauses, sips from the stone bird bath. In delight, icy remnants from my frigid winter heart instantly melt.

Before the sun swelters, I visit the garden to rake its rich, black blanket. A musty scent envelops me as I clear its flesh of unwanted weeds. Foxgloves glisten with morning's dew, their leaves lush green cups tending precious teardrops. Beyond, the bay glimmers like a trillion dancing diamonds to summon my presence. I wander down, pail in hand, wide brim hat adorning strawberry strands. Blackberries, plump, juicy, hang on prickly vines and beckon my fingers to free them.

As twilight turns we listen to the chorus of crooning crickets, mesmerized by their rhythm. From white wicker chairs we survey the sky for each glimmering star's appearance; for the moon to grace us with her presence. We stay until our halfmoon hangs suspended against a black satin sky. An image of this flawless moment embeds itself in heart like a rare, treasured photo.

All too soon maple's leaves rust subtly at the edges, while frost bites at the air. My reluctant heart sinks into a state of melancholy as autumn whispers her arrival. And yet, autumn weaves a magical web around me, capturing my spirit with threads of orange, rust and gold. The aroma of pungent apples and pears permeates autumn's air while Old Man Winter lurks in shadows like a thief in the night. Furry friends forage between maple's fallen leaves for their winter's hoard. Hunkering down in the kitchen, I preserve on cue, cramming the pantry like the squirrels and jays burying nuts in the garden.

I sense winter's wind skulking in the valleys of distant hills. Flames from autumn's evening fire throw eerie reflections on walls like dancing summer ghosts. Though I bask within the warmth of flames and spirit companionship, Old Man Winter taunts, whimpering, wavering in the shadows ....

September's Sun

September's sun
descends gently
     casts a bronze glow
     like gold-dust, at rest
on distant mountain shoulders

Slits
of hot pink cloud
streak
across twilight skies
like strips of ribbon
elongated
     their lustre allures
     to gift with grace
a fleeting embrace
from the outstretched arms
of an aching, bleeding, melting heaven

September's sun, spent
swallowed by horizons west
     sinks - in sacrifice
to soothe
a stretching, yawning, insatiable sea

Mountain Mist

wisps of white mist
sluggishly roll
to rest in mountain crevices
      like floating feathers
then leisurely
drift,
swathing alders, evergreens
before swallowing them whole

the mist stirs
with motion as gentle as a slow dance;
I hunger
for a ghostly embrace,
for this blanket of fog to engulf me
within its waltz;
I ache
for this wafting haze
to swoop, capture
cloak me:
to lay hidden within her calm cocoon
safely veiled,
a womb
      from the world,
      from humanity; her wild pulse,
oh, ethereal bed
fold me within,
sagely shroud me, soothe me
with silence and shadows...

Times Lost and Found

As the youngest of four children, offspring of a WWII Veteran and an English war bride, I missed all the beginnings in our family. I missed the firsts of absolutely everything, unless you want to count the shared Sunday bath brigade (alas, I date myself). As the youngest, I was last always, in every way. At times, my next older sister and I were seemingly not only last, but in addition, the forgotten children. Like a scruffy Raggedy Ann, almost everything I owned as a child was handed down from sisters of various ages, shapes and sizes.

Then, at the innocent age of four or five, I stumbled on a family fact so blatantly obvious to all others: my mother was absent from our tribe. I had spied an exquisite looking teapot on the top shelf of Granny's old wooden china cabinet.

"It's pretty, Granny."

"What's pretty, Tisha?"

"That, up there." I pointed to the pot.

Kindly indulging me, she opened the cabinet, picked up the pot and gently set it down on the kitchen table so I could carefully adore it while sitting in Grandpa's big captain's chair.

The glossy teapot was crafted in the image of an old-fashioned southern belle and apple green in color. Lacey layers of floor-length skirt formed the teapot body. A delicately chiseled face with hair swept high in elegant style crowned a graceful neckline and ruffle-strewn shoulders which molded the lid.

"It was your Mother's teapot, Tisha. One day, when you are a big girl, I shall give it to you to keep."

Questions sprang like rusty pipes busting leaks.

"My mother? Who is she? Where does she live?"

"In England," said Granny.

"Where is England?"

"A long way away. Across the ocean."

"Why does she live in England? Why doesn't she come

25

to see us? Will I ever see her again?"

Poor old Granny! She tried her best with explanations, but I was much too young to understand. Unable to connect the dots, I could not seem to comprehend a person never known or not remembered. My take-away was that most other children had mothers (whatever that meant) and mine lived way far away, and that she owned this shiny teapot. When I was as big as my neighbor Betty Ann, who lived across the street, the pot would be mine to treasure.

Back then, there were no pictures of my mother displayed at my grandparent's home. So how could I have known? Photographs of my mother surfaced much later in life, after my eldest sister married and left home. Sporadically, black and white photos began appearing – a portrait of my father in his army attire – our parents on their wedding day (Dad in uniform). These were formal shots. A few Polaroids surfaced as well. One of these was Mom posing in a dark, knee-length fur coat and a cloche hat, looking rather chic. Another was an impromptu shot of my parents strolling down a Vancouver street together arm in arm, dressed in winter coats, she with a strange-looking kerchief wrapped around her hair somewhat reminiscent of an *I Love Lucy* episode. One snapshot I possess today is a black and white of my parents on a warm summer day. The two are gazing intently into one another's eyes with smiles that can only be described as smoldering. I've been informed that the bulge in her belly was me.

From childhood I recall seeing my eldest sister's portrait on display. The image of a professionally taken 8" by 10" black and white profile is still clearly embedded in my mind's eye. Chestnut braids fell just past Ashley's shoulders, satin ribbons adorned the ends, straight-edged bangs crossed her forehead. She was doll-like, so girlish and pretty. Her eyes were big, bright, and she posed with the sweetest half-smile. A scar trailing down from the bottom edge of her right eyebrow was plainly visible (a fairly recent wound at the time). The blemish did not detract from portrayed innocence. Her appearance was angelic, adorable.

My older brother Aaron also had his childhood portrait taken. What an imp! Such a tiny little guy, cute as the dickens sporting a sailor hat and matching sailor's suit. His smile wide, eyes mischievous and freshly scrubbed, shining cheeks. He looked lovable and cuddly.

There were no portraits taken of Annabelle and I. When did we notice we were missing? We had obviously endured the babyhood and toddler years and survived. We surely had many typical childhood experiences. And yet, there were no outstanding instances nor vivid memories for us to draw upon. We were always left wondering, "What did we look like as babies?" Seemingly, our childhoods consisted of a myriad of elapsed occasions and forgotten days. Holes and gaps existed where mothers, memories and moments captured might have been. And as life marched on, questions fell by the wayside, or lapsed on dusty shelves.

Time kept slipping by. The remnants of my immediate family, like wounded soldiers, lamely and stoically marched off to separate battle grounds. Emotionally crippled from years of dysfunction, each shouldered gunny sacks filled with ghosts, secrets and skeletal remains. We carried our disfigured souls and stumbled upon land mines or front-lines of battlefields where we either waged war or became paralyzed prisoners in our quest and struggle to survive.

* * *

In my 50th year I was very much occupied with a career in bank management. I received an unexpected call at work one day, just after 5:00 PM. It was a cousin of mine I very rarely see or hear from, even though we were tight as kids.

"Tish, it's Jim. I have something you want. You need to drop by and pick it up."

"What do you mean? Where are you, Jim?"

"I'm over at Kate's. I can't tell you what is it. Trust me. You'll want it."

"When? I'm still at work."

"Come now. I'm leaving tomorrow for Calgary."

To say I was curious is an understatement. In spite of the mound of incomplete paperwork and phone messages, I tidied my desk and went through routine motions of closing and locking the branch for the day. I fled the office like a bandit in a getaway car with no idea what I was in for, but the message was clear – something I wanted.

En route to cousin Kate's I made one stop to purchase a bottle of red wine – an appreciation gift for Jim, or possibly a beverage to be consumed on site.

"Hey Jim! It's good to see you!"

After hugs were duly exchanged, I pounced on him. "So... what's up?"

While he went about setting up the television for DVD play, Jim explained that he had dropped by my father's house for a visit a couple of years back. My father had given Jim an old reel of film to see if he could do something with it. Dad offered that he had no idea what was on the film, but thought it was quite likely family events. Cousin Jim, more technically adept than I, had finally managed to transfer the film onto a DVD with music added for special effects.

A vaguely familiar-looking little girl suddenly appeared on the screen. A petite, shy little waif with freckles and a half-smile looked timid and uncertain with the scene unfolding around her. According to the cake candles, it was her fourth birthday. Wearing an old, ill-fitting bathing suit, her unkempt hair fell over her face, shielding her eyes as she coyly and inquisitively opened a box. She held up the gift contents: a pair of panties four times too big for her!

A tenor saxophone belts out an old tune from those times, a forgotten melody whose name I can almost – yet not quite – retrieve. It's on the tip of my tongue, but it doesn't matter in the next moment, because the camera's lens is now on the rest of the clan. My lord, how young they are! My dad, sisters, brother, grandparents, cousins, aunts and uncles are all there! Black and white film spews its reel, fluid images that capture hand stands, bites of hot dogs, jogging struts for the camera's lens. Granny pulls a little red wagon toting the youngest unidentifiable grandchild. As each new face appears on the scene, recognition springs.

"Bobby! Duane! Sally! Who on earth is that?"

"Uncle Dan ... oh my God, look – it's Kerry-Ann!" Jim laughs.

Suddenly we are transported to a lake. Cars parked in the vicinity are circa 1940s and 50s. I'm pint-sized in my bathing suit, splashing water, sitting on the wooden step of a small dock with two other children I don't remember. A frightening memory from this event springs to mind but there's no time to ponder it because now scenes from my grandparents' 50th wedding anniversary are underway. Each set of aunts, uncles and my grandparents are all dressed up in their Sunday best, waltzing. A band plays in the background behind the dancing couples. My Dad (who is part of the band) blows his saxophone. What I'm hearing, though, is canned 'big band' blaring away. Words land on the tip of my tongue and roll off: "Don't sit under the apple tree ... with anyone else but me ... anyone else but me ... anyone else but me ... no, no, no. "

A Christmas scene in Granny's living room flashes before us. Dad and my eldest sister are mostly evident, she's bossing with hands on hips. I glimpse myself in pajamas in the background, but the image is gone in an instant. Abruptly, many of the clan are seated around the kitchen table. There I am, sitting in a grown-up chair, my chin barely reaching high enough to touch the table.

"Look how little she is!" I cry out.

The film swings into another family gathering at my grandparents', but much later in life.

"Julie!"

"Linda!"

"Mrs. Olsen!"

There are little tykes I don't know. This footage had

to occur in the '70s as evidenced by a few of my long-haired, mustached cousins. Quite likely I had long fled the remnants of nest in search of adventure and my place in the world.

In the space of three to five minutes, the film finishes. The TV screen is blank. I'm simultaneously sad and ecstatic. Self-consciously, I realize my eyes have become spigots for tears and I am holding in muted sobs. Of joy? I am overwhelmed, awed, delighted, dismayed.

"Play it again, Jim," I command.

He appeases me again and again. Each time the reel runs, it reveals something new, or someone else we identify. We point and exclaim, "Glenda!" or "Aaron!"

Finally, when I have had my fill of the show for that particular moment in time, the words I eventually spew are terribly awkward, so inadequate. How does one thank someone for such a bewildering gift, a gift of times lost and found? A grown woman, a once-forgotten child, now in possession of a newly-found image to tuck inside my mind's eye – yet all I can manage to muster is a river of tears.

Today, on occasion, I will take down that DVD, insert it into the player and revisit those times lost and found. Each time I discover something new. And every so often, I dust off my southern belle teapot which takes me back in time to Granny's kitchen. Each time I dust her, my lady's apple green sheen seems to glow just a little more brightly.

Mother and Son

they built castles
in the sand
          mother and son
a bright green pail
four hands
two hearts

an old black crow
lurked nearby
watching, waiting, surveying
like some inquisitive bystander

in the absence of crumbs
I found myself pondering
did he wait
for the finished fortress?
unearth clams?
          or perhaps
this wise old bird
simply wished to bear witness
          and dine
on
joy

Love

Love ambled
hand in hand
along sandy shores

hand in hand
it sauntered towards the distant sea
as wave upon wave rolled forward
in welcome

I watched
as love - four feet
in perfect rhythm - crept closer
to water's edge
       two specks on the horizon
until
the span of sand
stretched
to the point where
unified,
       it appeared as one
and the waves washed
love's debut
       in baptism

Footsteps

Have you ever arranged a trip abroad in haste, boarded the flight to endure twelve grueling hours in the air with a flying phobic seated adjacent to you, then arrive at your destination wondering "What am I doing here?"

I'm still asking myself this, even now, standing in this odd and unfamiliar English funeral home. I comprehend this is Guildford, a small market town about half-way between London and Portsmouth in the south of England – but it's almost surreal. This viewing parlor is explicitly designed with grieving families in mind. Small, private, it provides opportunity to mourn over the body, pay last respects, say good-byes. Here, family alone is able to share sorrow and mourn prior to the public chapel service and burial ritual.

So I view her. It's what I'm supposed to do. I've been to funerals in the past, but I've not seen a dead body before. The open, oblong casket rests on a stretcher-like table. The folds of white satin lining the inside of the casket give an impression of clouds sheathing her stilled body. With eyelids closed, her face appears almost serene, as if she's only asleep. Her shock of white hair seems the same style as in her last photo, wavy strands combed straight back off the face. With such a pale complexion the freckles seem to pop. She's still attractive, in spite of age, in spite of illness, in spite of death's call.

I'm supposed to feel something, I know. Regret, or anguish. Perhaps gnawing emotional pain; maybe what I'd feel over a lost limb or pierced heart. Tears should spill in torrents. Like Beth, in the corner.

Red splotches encase her turquoise eyes. Wet, flushed cheeks are clearly visible. I dig deep, attempting to summon up some appropriate emotion. Surely to God there must be something here. Perhaps just under the surface, a volcanic well awaits to erupt. Yet nothing emerges. A hollow abyss, I stand perfectly still. Quiet. Respectful. Silently, I intimate to the rigid corpse before me, "Good-bye, Mother. May God be with you."

I'm embarrassed. For her. For me. There should be more. Much more.

* * *

After the viewing, we cram together like matchsticks in my step-father Daniel's tiny car and head towards the family home. But there, it too is cramped, cold and uncomfortable. Beth makes tea as the rest of us assemble in the living room, clustering around heat grates which are only turned on intermittently. The room is box-like and contains a faded plaid sofa and worn arm chairs to accommodate five adults and a teenager.

My eldest sister, Ashley, does most of the talking, as always. I observe, speak when spoken to, as normal. Beth, the oldest of my mother's second set of children is, apparently, the family's mouth-piece. She shares agonizing details. We hear of Mother's illness, the pain, specific aspects of her suffering, the moment of death.

I reflect on the finality of her death. The lack of impact on me is disconcerting, and yet all I ever knew of my mother while growing up was the odd birthday card signed "love Mum." Once, an ocean-side photograph of her along side a young girl was enclosed in a card. This was my introduction to the existence of my half-sister, Beth, and two half-brothers, Brian and Kenny. I have no real memories of Mother to speak of, save one. All I knew about my mother were second-hand details disclosed from older sibling's memories, or the occasional jibe from my emotionally distant father. His bitterness never strayed far from the tip of his tongue. I wonder, again, why we were informed of her death, yet not her illness.

Beth persists in her English drawl: "Cancer, the cause of death, technically. But I think, in the end, it was really the guilt that killed her."

"Oh Beth, get on with you," pipes Kenny, the youngest, flashing a smile.

Mother's husband Daniel concedes that it is a point to consider. Brian remains mute. I don't think Brian has uttered two words since we've arrived. I've never met such a rigid, distant young man before. Upon embracing him, as I supposed half-siblings should, it felt like hugging a tree trunk. He's been sullen ever since. I believed him to be grieving, but now I'm not so sure.

"What do you mean, Beth?" I find my voice.

"Well, you know – guilt. From the past. Leaving you all behind there, in Canada."

"Really?"

"Well, I think so. She talked about you all non-stop when the boys and I were growing up. I believe it just ate away at her. You know. The guilt." Beth pauses to light a cigarette, draws deeply.

Surprised, I ponder this idea. Perhaps her various addictions I'd been told about were a coping mechanism for guilt?

"You know, she may have left you all behind in Canada, but she also abandoned us. In other ways," Beth states.

"Oh? How so?" Ashley asks.

"Well, you see, Brian, Kenny and I were shipped off to boarding schools. Right Dad?"

"Your mother simply couldn't cope with too many children, Beth. You know she loved you all, though," he answers.

Brian straightens the flex in his back. Icy blue eyes throw daggers at Beth as he rises and leaves the room without a word. Kenny tosses his red waves back, laughing, "What's wrong with boarding school? I think it's a hoot!"

I keep silent as my thoughts drift to the abortions my own father alluded to in the past. A count of three English offspring, four left in Canada, and two forsaken before birth equals nine babies. For someone who 'couldn't cope with too many children,' that's substantial. I blush mutely at my judgment before empathy sets in – that times were different.

I'm barren by choice. I imagine birth control was not readily available during the war years and later. Catholic faith, and alcoholism, quite likely contributed to unplanned events and indiscretions. In light of this new information, though, I consider for the first time that as challenging as life was with my father in Canada, it could have been worse. At least he kept us four together. Mostly.

* * *

Like a scene from a foreign movie, the old English chapel's grey stonework is weathered and worn almost smooth. A quaint graveyard situated just beyond the chapel registers as unusual to me. Canadian cemeteries I've known are separate from the church, massive and well-manicured. Here, long green grass clumps between tombstones of various sizes, shapes and ages. These headstones eerily present as phantom monuments; they haphazardly litter the landscape. The chapel's heavy oak door embedded with cast iron hinges and a protruding cross signifies the entrance. A priest greets us as we enter, falling into a hallway crammed tight with boxes, crates and white sheets draped over larger mystery articles.

"You must forgive us. I'm afraid we've renovations underway," Father McKay conveys. He guides us to a small chapel where the service is to be held. "Please make yourselves comfortable – I'll be with you straight away."

An ornate stained glass window hangs high above the right wall of this tiny cathedral. Light from outside filters softly through a mosaic of rose, amber, turquoise and emerald green. The left wall contains a window comprised of intricate leaded-glass panes, offering a glimpse of the cemetery beyond. A dozen wooden pews, varnish-worn and pock-marked from years of use, fills up the chapel space. Six pews to the left, six right. A cross bearing the image of crucified Christ is mounted high on the slatted wall, behind the altar, which sits front and centre. The pulpit faces us from the left.

A minute before the service begins, I can't help but notice how few are here. Ashley and I, representing Mother's Canadian offspring, sit in the second pew. Mother's husband, Daniel, fills the front pew along with Beth, Brian and Kenny. Only two others are present, mature ladies, wearing old-fashioned black-veiled hats and reeking of dusting powder. A nauseating scent of intermingled lilac and lavender permeates the air. Father McKay's robes swish and sway, breaking the silence as he enters the chapel and takes his place at the pulpit.

"Welcome, family and friends of Emily Carson who has recently and regrettably passed. Regrettably I say ... given those of you she leaves behind to mourn her death."

Father McKay begins to drone about Mother's life, and provides pieces of history and personal details no doubt shared beforehand by Daniel.

Bring, Bring
Bring, Bring
Bring Bring

The ring of a telephone is piercing, intrusive. Its shrillness resonates, as if the instrument is situated just outside the door, in the hallway. Surely, someone will get that.

Bring, Bring
Bring, Bring

"And here with us today are two of her children from Canada, Ashley and Tess. I'm sure Emily would be quite pleased."

Bring, Bring
Bring, Bring
Bring, Bring

"Other surviving children include Elizabeth, Brian and Kenneth."

Bring, Bring
Bring, Bring

Internally, I roar "Will someone GET THAT?"
Bring, Bring
Bring, Bring
"Survived also by her loyal, loving husband, Daniel."
Bring, Bring
Bring, Bring

I no longer hear the hum of Father McKay's words. The telephone has violently invaded my psyche, distracting me. It's reminiscent of the recent midnight imposition, the fierce clanging of the phone at my bedside awakening me in a panic from a deep slumber. Ashley's voice on the other end, "Tess, Mom's died. I have to go back."

Attention now clearly diverted, I glance outside the paned window on the left wall. My eyes nearly leap from my skull. Two grave diggers loiter beneath a lone oak tree in the cemetery. One man hunches in a small excavator, the other leans on his shovel, hands gloved. Shooting the breeze, they wait. Wait to complete the task at hand. Obvious. Oblivious.
Bring, Bring
Bring, Bring

A tear, at long last, surfaces from within. Slowly, silently, it slides down my cheek.

* * *

After arriving back in Canada, life returned to normal for Ashley and I, she, busy raising two children, while I worked in a bank and navigated the stormy seas of a tumultuous marriage. Before long, I left my husband. Rather hastily, I located a dingy basement suite to rent, and picked up the remnants of heart and self from the dust of divorce dealings. Only twenty-five, I was intent on getting on with the task of living. Something else had changed, though, in addition to my marital status and domicile. Footsteps arrived.

Footsteps came to me at night. And yet, not every night. Periodically, footsteps sounding light in the distance would grow louder as they approached – stronger, stronger as they neared close, closer. Then abruptly, they stopped. Stopped always right beside my bed. The first time the footsteps came, I presumed this intruder would rape, then murder me. But not a finger was laid on me, even as my heart attempted to jump from my chest. When the pounding eventually subsided, I'd listen intently for the footsteps' retreat. Silence. Subsequently, when the footsteps returned again – and again – I'd always listen. I'd listen for them to depart, or for a voice to softly whisper. Instead, always I'd hear my own heart brutally beating. They'd come. They remained speechless. Never would they leave.

I came to believe this basement was haunted by the ghost of a previous dweller. Perhaps I now lay where her possessive spirit used to rest. And yet, these footsteps did not come to just this one bed. Eventually, I met a new man and moved away to try my luck at love again. Footsteps continued to come to me occasionally, always at night, immediately after tucking in, prior to sleep enveloping me.

When footsteps came there, I'd ask my new man, Ron, "Did you hear them?"

"Hear what?"

"The footsteps."

"You must be dreaming."

"But I'm not sleeping. I JUST went to bed!"

Once, visiting with my sister overnight, having just said goodnight, the footsteps came, and stopped, right beside where I lay on her sofa.

"Ashley?" I called out to the black of the night. Echoes of my own voice and stillness the only reply.

* * *

A delightful surprise has arrived this autumn afternoon. Snow, in October! Snow! I can't wait to feel the frozen flecks on my face. Bundling in layers of sweaters, I quickly don a scarf, winter jacket and boots. Setting out for a walk, the destination is undetermined until I arrive. From a dull, grey sky the snow slides down, dusting trees, creating feather-like leaves and drooping boughs. The lake swallows the plump flakes. Thick fluff, like white cotton balls is falling, falling, falling from the heavens. Statue-like, I'm captivated by this spectral flurry, feet firmly rooted. Mesmerized, my trance-like thoughts drift with the snowfall. A long forgotten memory descends between snowflakes. Gently it lands. The sound of footsteps, so many years ago approaching a toddler in a crib. A warm, fragrant body embraces me, weeps, then the footsteps fade. The footsteps vanish down an endless hall.

The snow is soft, cool against my skin, now pink, as numbness wraps me. White crystals falling, falling. They blanket Mother Earth, burying her deeper, deeper until her rich, black flesh is concealed. Leaving the icy bleakness of the lake, my solitary tracks are clearly visible. Retracing the prints, homeward bound, comes the recognition that haunting footsteps will finally cease. Steps will retreat, be stilled, silenced. At last they will mutely rest in an overgrown graveyard which lays adjacent to an old and distant English Chapel.

Rock Her

ocean's chant
a rhythm
to rock her,
softly it splashes
          a lullaby
to stroke
soothe
hush
the wail within,
          like salve
upon singed skin

rocking horse waves
lull
silence
          still
the echoes

each ripple
rocks her, rocks her,
she rides each swell
inching nearer
the horizon
the place where sun sinks into sea
gateway
          to heaven's distant door

Dear Mother,

I'm living in an exquisite corner of Earth reserved especially for me. Sounds strange, I know, but true. Daniel Point beckoned my spirit from a distance. The moment I rounded the bend in Lee Bay, well ... heart leaped up to clutch my throat. Instantaneously, Mother, I perceived tides rushing, reaching, to capture my ebbing spirit. Nature, pure, rare, yielding an artist's palette of changing views; intuitively, implicitly, my destiny was determined.

One day, Mother, waters are still and glassy as I pass by Mixel Lake. Pristine treed mountains are reflected in mirror-like image beneath clear, azure skies. The next day a front moves in. Skies turn heavy, laden with thick white billows. Thin wisps of cloud lay in cedar boughs and mountain crevices, lazy, melting marshmallows. Mist hovers, rests ghost-like on Mixel's plane. Sometimes, I think I see your spirit drifting with the mist.

Closer to home, one day the bay glitters like a trillion fallen, floating stars; the next, white caps race to catch one another. Days march on. Seasons come; seasons pass. And yet, each day brings a fresh canvas and a brand new palette of paint.

Mother, at times I linger on sun-bleached driftwood at the ocean's edge. Here, I let the sun wash over me, warm me. I listen to the rhythm of the waves. Gently they roll, infinitely sequential, like a pulse softly splashing against the rocky bluff. Their tempo gives rise to a symphony. Seagulls, as chorus, join this composition. A range of melancholic cries echo as they circle high.

I rise at dawn each day. Gradually, nature's designs unveil before me. Like a mystery novel, her clues obscured, she waits to be unearthed, unravelled, discovered; secrets ache to be shared like loons that fly east in early morning skies. Their stride, their lonely lament aligns in pace with my pulsing heart. Chattering, scavenging squirrels scurry about, eagles screech and scout for prey. Deer meander and quietly graze, inquisitive, yet skittish if I move too quickly. Mother, here at Daniel Point you can hear dew as it drops to quench earth's thirst and the whoosh, whoosh, whoosh of ravens' wings in flight overhead. My trembling aspen shivers with delight as just a whisper of wind caresses its leaves. Its rustling lulls me, stills my mind like the calm upon lake waters.

As sun melts into the ocean, a sinking scarlet sphere, the chorus of crickets croon beneath a blushing violet glow. Their secret so simple; their song mystifies, captivates my dancing spirit. Twilight turns. I scan indigo skies for a glimpse of evening's first star. One night, Mother, perhaps I shall visit you there. For now, as each glimmering diamond emerges on centre stage, heart sings. I'm here, Mother, cocooned. I am the enchanted dweller of Daniel Point. My pulse catches its rhythm and merges with the sea, the sounds, the stillness, the seasons.

When the student is ready, Mother, the teacher arrives.

Stillness

stillness
opens me
like blossoms unfolding;
my gaping heart
gathers up
morning's mist
as it weaves between leaves
and lingers in bows of cedar
that lie
like open arms, their evergreen scent
subdued
by traces of burning firewood
and fresh bouquet of lilac

nearby, low tide
reveals sea's secrets,
starfish
like miniature suns;
minnows whose feeding frenzy resembles raindrops;
mussels, in intimate clusters cling
to pilings, like a tight-knit clan

gulls glide, circle, cry
oh, how they cry, cry, cry
to haunt me at the core
as spirit
stilled,
raises its hand and strokes, soothes, brushes heart
as if to say,
be still, be still
and know
I am

The Arrival of Joy

Sorrow
strolled
shedding tears
like morning dew
     yet sipped
from the cup of Spring:
a cloudless sky
a sapphire-sea;
     drew breaths
of honeyed lilac, sweet grass,
and the scent of seaweed.

Sorrow sauntered
swallowed
sea birds' songs
     drank in sprays of waves
as they splashed and raced to shore.
Ocean's breeze
stroked Sorrow's skin - now stilled
as a lone otter
chewed its catch in the bay beyond
     then rolled
sank
without a ripple
received
by the sea.
As Sorrow slipped below sea's horizon
to surpass a grove of green,
Spring's newborn leaves
     gently waved
     like emerald flags
and
as Sorrow
rounded a jewel-strung bended path

the light step
of Joy
skipped home.

Florence Walker

Has been writing since she was a child and her artistic career spans 20+ years. As one of the founders of Art Friends of Halifax, Nova Scotia, some of her words were brought to life by actors on the stage in a story about the war brides of Halifax.

Florence has studied at the Nova Scotia College of Art and Design, as well as with a number of well-known BC artists and writers. Along with writing and painting, Florence is a quilter, baker, gardener and chef extraordinaire!

Currently, Florence is working on three projects:

Katie Ann: Who Am I? – creative nonfiction;

Creations from the Musings of her Mind – a series of humorous stories which speak to both vulnerability and resilience;

The Dreamtime Adventures – illustrations for a children's book.

Gulf of
St. Lawrence

Red River

Pleasant Bay

CAPE BRETON
HIGHLANDS
NATIONAL PARK

Presqu'ile

Chéticamp
Petit Étang
Belle-Marche

Point Cross

Grand Étang

St Joseph du Moine

Cap Le Moine

Kingross

Margaree Harbour Bell Cote

219

Chimney Corner

Portree

East
Margaree

Margaree
Centre

Margaree
Valley

Egypt Road

St Rose

Margaree
Forks

North East
Margaree

Cape Breton
Island

Dunvegan

Southwest
Margaree

Lake
O'Law

Finlayson

Inverness

Upper Margaree

19

Upper
Middle River

Middle River

North River Bridge

St Anns

N Gut St Anns

South Gut
St Anns

Forks
Baddeck

Big Hill

Big
Bay

Northumberland
Strait

Strathlorne

Scotsville

Lower
Middle River

205

Mabou Mines

Black River

Lake
Ainslie
East Side

Hunters
Mountain

Baddeck

Mabou Harbour Mouth

Mason
Point

305

Trout River

Nyanza

Wagmatcook

Washabuck
Centre

Shunaca

W Mabou Harbour

Mabou

Glenville

252

Lake Ainslie
South Side

Bucklaw

St Andrews Channel

Port Hood

Brook
Village

Churchview

Little Narrows

McKinnons
Harbour

Iona

Christmas Island

Eskasoni

Glencoe
Station

Glencoe
Mills

Whycocomagh

Estmere

223

Grand
Narrows

216

Big

Maryville

Upper
SW Mabou

Blues Mills

West Alba

Judique

Orangedale

Big Harbour Island

Middle Cape

Campbell

Valley
Mills

Malagawatch

Militia Point

Irish Cove

Saler
Roa

Glendale

River Denys

Marble
Mountain

Bras d'Or Lake

Johnstown

Lake List

Craigmore

Kingsville

Lime Hill

Cape
George
Harbour

Red Islands

Hay Cove

St Georges
Bay

19

West Bay
Road

St Georges
Channel

McNab Cove

Creignish

Queensville

West Bay

Dundee

French Cove

Chapel Island

Soldiers Cove

Havre Boucher

4

Troy

Cleveland

McIntyre
Lake

Sporting
Mountain

St Peter's

Barra Head

Grand River

Frankville
Linwood
Acadie

Aulds
Cove

Port
Hastings

Grantville
Lineauville

Grande
Anse

4

River
Bourgeois

L'Ardoise

Grande Greve

47

MULGRAVE

43

45

104

46

Grandique
Louisdale

D'Escousse

217

Point Mc

Monastery

Mattie
Settlement

Point Tupper

HAWKESBURY

Lr River Inhabitants

Lennox

320

INVERNESS

VICTORIA

Indian Bro

Tarbotvale

Bras d'Or Lake Channel

Lennox Passage

48

Katie Ann

1886 - 1923

Resembling a bent and broken old spruce, Katie Ann swaggered through the knee-high snow drifts lugging two buckets of water. Years before, in the early 1800s, the old folks dug the well much closer to the livestock barn than to the house, almost a quarter mile away. The thick wool scarf not only protected her from the bitter nor'easter blasting up the hill, but also hid the twisted grimace on her face. It was thirty below and the winds were blowing hard, a typical Cape Breton gale.

"Ios, Ios, Muire Bhan," she muttered. Jesus, Jesus, Virgin Mary.

Tonight her thoughts were just as bitter. Still, she took a minute to stop and catch her breath, and as she swallowed the crystal air, she looked up into the heavens, all purple and luminous with the moon near full, and sighed deeply. Yes, she expected the final decision had been made. They'd be leaving at the end of the week. Again, her thoughts wandered for a minute and she swore under her breath, "Ios, Muire Bhan, Ios, Muire Bhan. How will I ever make do?"

It had taken her over a week now, sorting through their few meager belongings, the bits she still actually owned. The weariness dragged her down so. She half expected to collapse on the spot. Staring off over the glen, even at eight o'clock in the evening, the moon's illumination seemed to lift up the silhouettes of the shadows from the crosses below. She counted six graves in all. Parts of her family, parts of herself, lost forever.

Katie Ann noticed some of the crosses were half-buried under the snow, and as she stood there on this freezing November night in 1923, she wished she had made the time to tend them in the proper manner. 'Maybe I'll get back to them in the spring,' she hopes.

"Move on now and stop your moping before you freezes yourself to death," she mumbles.

As she approached the top of the hill, Katie Ann could hear the ruckus caused by her four children before she entered the back porch. The old wooden buckets she carried had long since overflowed and measured just over half full. This would have to do til morning when one of the boys would help get what was needed to start the day. She hung her snow-laden scarf and coat on the peg nailed to the back of the door as she outstretched her foot to haul over the three-legged stool. Plunking herself down, she tugged on her boots' metal clasps, frozen stiff with slush and ice. Banging her heels on the floorboards, the black rubber gumboots came away from her long narrow feet. As she rolled down her old, gray socks she saw they needed mending, again. Pretty soon they would be more mend than sock.

She lifted herself from the stool, aware that the noise behind the kitchen door was getting louder. Or was it simply her tiredness that made it seem so? "Ios, Ios, Ios," she grumbled. She gave the door a hard crack with her fist. The door flung open and instant silence ensued under her sullen mood.

It didn't take long before the water was hauled over to the kettle and poured in to warm for the night wash-up. Half muttering, tight-lipped, Katie Ann couldn't keep from gritting her teeth at the sight of her children. *They look as if they are frightened of me.* "Yuss get on now. Stop gratin' on the bit of patience I got left."

They all gobbled their bannock and dark molasses. Florence, the oldest, trying to help her mother, saw to the washing up: a quick scrub of their faces and hands then she gathered together her sister and two brothers and shooed them from the kitchen. "To bed, to bed we go."

Standing in the now quiet kitchen, Katie Ann found little solace. By and by she found herself drifting off into her own world. Her anger ate away at her, robbing her of the chance of at least some tiny relief. "After all," she spit out the words, "He is dead and gone isn't he. I'm free of it. It's over."

Her thoughts continued to drift to that whole, seemingly endless, period of exhaustion; of pain and of giving, giving, giving to a husband who only knew how to take. Right up to his last gasp for breath, she was slave to his never-ending, demanding wants and sullying needs. As she glanced in the direction of the stove, she could still see the old cot stuck out from behind where he spent the last three years of his life. She could still feel his intrusive presence as a shiver of shame passed through her body.

"What is a wife really supposed to be, anyway?" she asked herself. "I'm glad it's ended. Never again will I put myself under the bidding of a man."

The kettle steamed and the aroma of the black tea leaves filled her with comfort as she poured the water into the dented silver teapot. She loved this teapot, a wedding gift from her sister, Flora, all the way from the Boston States. Flora was ten years younger than Katie Ann. Smarter too, by all accounts, Katie Ann thought. Her mind wandered: 'Maybe someday I'll go there too.' She stood still for a while, feeling the heat from the cast iron wood stove seep into her body, warmth at the end of this unhappy day.

After pouring a mug of strong brew, she dragged her chair over, lowering herself onto it. She threw the tattered old shawl from the back of her chair onto the open oven door and slowly raised her feet to rest upon the shawl. The tea was so, so good, and for the first time in nearly sixteen years she found herself steeped in thoughts alien and personal-like. Thoughts of herself – just Katie Ann, the woman.

"Och, indeed," she muttered. "It was allays this way, as far back as I let myself t'ink. I feel the same still."

As she sat, she began to fidget. She was no longer comfortable before the stove. Still, she remained, and despite her indignation, the past crept in. She couldn't hide from her own shame; felt as though she'd denied her whole existence up til now. It had all happened so fast. "How could I be blaming myself? For wasn't it my father who made the big mistake?" No matter which way she went at it, she came to the same ending: right here, in this scandalous situation, she had lost her home.

Seamus MacDonnell had been a second generation descendent of early immigrants to Canada from Invernesshire, Scotland in the 1800s. Seamus' father had managed to hold onto the few acres allotted him by the Nova Scotia government. When his father died, Seamus was only forty, and, as the eldest son, inherited the small family holdings. Known as a different sort, he was so bound and determined to be successful that the traditional tendencies seemed far too old-fashioned for him. He did not encourage his siblings, two brothers and a sister, to stay home on the farm. The two brothers went off to the woods in Maine with their friends and became lumberjacks while his sister married at a very young age and moved to Port Hood.

Back then, Katie Ann figured, her father had had his own ideas. He needed a wife and wanted his own family. He had ambitions. When almost everyone in the county married his own cousin, sometimes even first cousins, Seamus decided not to marry by the ways of the times. No, instead, he married a tiny bit of a girl named Flora MacLellan. Actually, Flora wasn't really of the MacLellan clan, so therefore MacLellan wasn't even her real name.

Katie Ann stretched to grab the handle of the old tea pot, remembering with a sense of nostalgia how many times she had poured tea from other old kettles steeped over this very stove. "Och, indeed! I shouldn't be lamenting now, should I? After all, I can't change the past," she heard herself saying. "I allays figured my own mother wept enough for ten women, being such a sullen and rather shy t'ing."

As Katie Ann's memories overflowed, she could see her mother, the first Flora, baking bread over the low counter, built that way to suit her short stature. When Seamus MacDonnell had announced he'd take Flora MacLellan for his wife, many a spinster in the area was insulted - even outraged - that he would ever think of doing such a thing. After all, whoever heard the like? Such a good catch in so many ways, handsome and a landowner as well, to go and marry outside his own kind, and a Micmac Indian woman to boot! Despite what his neighbors thought of his soon-to-be wife, Seamus was set on following through.

Sadie, wife of Allan MacLellan, was a neighbour of Seamus MacDonnell. Needing help around the farm with the milking and planting and of course the minding of their brood of youngsters, Flora, a half-starved and destitute Micmac child of fourteen, had landed in the MacLellan home. The year was 1875, and Flora didn't want to live in the white folks' home. She would have preferred to stay with her own people, but they were starving on the Indian reservation and there were too many mouths to feed. She had no choice but to go outside to find work. She had no idea, at such a young age, how painful it would be.

The Micmac *(Mi'Kmag)* way was a unique lifestyle, much different from that of the white Scottish settlers who had invaded their territories generations before. From the very beginning, lie upon lie was spread about the Micmacs. By the time Flora was born, the Europeans had established that the indigenous peoples were "Savages," when in truth they were actually strong and loyal men, quick to greet in friendship and living with the belief that all men were equal.

As the years passed by, the native people came to totally mistrust the white men. Hence, it was a terrible blow when Flora left the reservation and entered under the roof of the white people. Too serious to be forgiven, Flora's own kin forbid her re-entry on the Chapel Island Reservation ever again. She was totally cut off from her family, a cruel burden to bear, still loving her people as she did.

Flora was actually a workhorse, not uncommon for most women then, especially women in service. Sadie named her Flora, not wanting to use her Indian name; but the truth was Sadie couldn't pronounce Flora's real name. It was an almost impossible task for Flora to follow Sadie's bidding, and all for a roof over her head and a bite to eat.

Of course it went without saying that Flora was pretty well rejected by the entire white community. Her isolation was extreme, and later she told her children how she always felt invisible to everyone. She was desperate for adult company for most of her life.

Och, indeed. I knows the legacy my mother left behind was that of resiliency, Katie Ann thought as she straightened her back to the chair.

She could still hear her father's very rare sharing, long after her mother had passed on, of how he came to marry Flora.

She had been just shy of sixteen when Seamus made known his intention to marry her. He had given his reasons: Flora was certainly not his cousin, and being an Indian, she'd keep to herself; she wouldn't be a bother to his progress; and she was a good worker.

However, even before the wedding between Flora and Seamus MacDonnell, everyone knew there were other problems. For starters, it wasn't lawful at that time for a white person to marry an Indian. Because Flora had to take the surname of her employer for legal purposes, the marriage certificate stated that Flora MacLellan and Seamus (James) MacDonnell married in the Gillisdale Catholic Church in May of 1877.

Here on this cold November night, Katie Ann remembered the gossiping neighbours, always gawking at her and her siblings and especially her mother, snickering whenever they showed up in the Gillisdale general store. How embarrassing it was for Flora's children, especially the girls, to be called dirty names like half-breed and squaw. Even today Katie Ann felt separate from these others, always without a place, not quite a real person. She still experienced a sense of deep humiliation: to this very day, Katie Ann's feelings of shame around her mother gripped at her gut. *Damn, damn, will I never be free of it?*

"Ios, Ios, how old am I anyway?" she questions herself now. "Yes, I was born Catherine Ann MacDonnell, July 8th, 1886 in Egypt, Inverness County, Cape Breton. I'm getting on to 36 years now. My mother bore eight children in all, and I'm the last of the five who survived."

Melting deeper into her chair, getting sleepy, Katie Ann continued musing. Her papa, Seamus, worked hard, and being frugal, succeeded in becoming a man of means. In the beginning, he worked in the woods, leaving home for the winter, saving every cent to put back into the farm. In the spring he'd purchase more cows and clear more acreage to be put to the plow. Upon the arrival of his second son, he no longer left his wife and children alone during the winters. His family stood to benefit from his years of toil. And indeed, all of Katie Ann's siblings certainly did fare well in the long run.

"All but me," she muttered under her breath now.

"Mamma, Mamma, what are you doing? It's so cold here in the kitchen. Get up now and let me bank up the stove for the night. Go on now – you're freezing yourself to death."

Florence's voice startled her out of her deep reminiscences. Heaving herself from the chair, Katie Ann felt the pins and needles shoot through her feet as they bore her weight, reminding her anew of the old injury to her right knee, an accident that had nearly crippled her as just a young girl. She'd been chopping the firewood and the ax missed its target and cut through to the bone. Somehow, it was her foot that suffered the damage. Rheumatism had set in.

"Ios, Ios, the foot's actin' up now. I hopes it don't keep me awake the night through," she said to the back of her eldest as she limped awkwardly toward the staircase.

She spent little time on her nightly habits. She took a trip to the chamber pot in the small closet off the upstairs hallway and quickly returned to her bedroom to throw a splash onto her face from the tin washbasin. So weary was she this night she could hardly pull up the heavy patchwork quilt to cover herself. Breathing a labored sigh of resignation, Katie Ann turned to her right side with her left hand feeling under her pillow for her black rosary beads.

"In the name of the Father, the Son and the Holy ...,"

were her last words before drifting off.

Rising the following morning, the weather still well below the zero mark, she knew that in another day all would be done. No more time for lamentations over being passed by or passed over. As Katie Ann stirred the porridge, she thought about her father again. Seamus wasn't a stupid man. As far as she could remember, he must have intended to do right by her. After all, she was the one who stayed home: even after her marriage she still planned to care for her father. "Och, how I used to dream of long peaceful days here on the old farm," she spoke under her breath. Having so few adults for company she often spoke to herself. "How I wish my sister Mae were here to talk out t'ings wit. Of course, she couldn't change t'ings any more than me."

For the millionth time Katie Ann tried to accept what her father had done. When it came right down to it, he wouldn't have believed how things had turned out. She spoke to herself again: "I can still remember the day he sat wit' me and told me that when he passed away, he'd be leaving everything he had to me, his favorite child."

And he did leave it all to her. And of course she deserved it after taking care of him the last years while he was almost bedridden. None of the others had helped at all; not the way she did, always trying harder to make things work.

"Too bad. When it came right down to it, he must have known the law." Katie Ann's voice rose: "He must have known that when a man married a woman, everything she had became his property. Ios, Ios, he should have written something in his last will and testament to protect me from losing it all." Again and again she battered herself with dark thoughts of doubts and shame.

When all was said and done, she had nothing. Nothing.

Hearing the four bairns come down the stairs, she muttered, "Damn, damn, here I am, so agitated with t'ings the breakfast cereal is all caught on the bottom of the pot, nearly burned. Och, they'll have to eat it anyway."

She loved her children as best she could. She watched them from the corner of her eye as she stood at the stove. Florence, the oldest, was a lot like herself, rather tall and with a certain proud way about her. Such a good girl, she already had the youngest three all dressed for the day. The littlest one, Jane, was just the most beautiful child for miles around. *Ah, surely it'll be better after a while,* Katie Ann thought.

She set the boys to chores in the barn. There was the wagon to be loaded and the wheels to be taken off, the cow to be tethered and other things to be fixed and made ready for travel. Katie Ann thought of her two sons: Joseph, the oldest, who she knew, even at thirteen years was trouble. He reminded Katie Ann of her oldest brother, surly and mean to everyone in his path. No, Joe-Hee, as she called him, wasn't going to have an easy go of it in life and God help the woman he married - if any woman would have him. And the younger of her two sons, James—called Jimmy Duncan or Jimmy-Dee by the family— just about seven years old now, a shy but willing boy, eager to please and help her whenever she bade him. She felt closer to him.

She turned from the stove as the blast of cold air carried the two of them into the kitchen. She noticed Jimmy-Dee had been crying and she gave him a pitying look, which quickly turned to a scowl as Joe-Hee dragged his wet feet across the kitchen, boots leaving a trail of muck and slush in his path. Katie Ann had just about quit trying to discipline the boy. Ignoring him she went to the foot of the stairs and called her girls down to breakfast.

"So, we got everything cleared from the two cupboards up in our room. How are we ever going to fit it all into those trunks?" Florence asked no one in particular. And Janie, the little one, so quick to laugh, stared at her sister and chuckled.

"We'll make tiny, tiny balls of things and mush them into the big wooden trunks. They'll fit. But I can just carry Annie and Jessie, my two little rag dolls. They won't take any room." Florence leaned over and hugged her sister, giving her a little wink.

Katie Ann finally took her place at the table, and closing her eyes for a few seconds said a word of thanks before taking a sip of her tea. Nothing much was said about the food – a bowl of porridge, a slice of thick bread and molasses and a glass of milk. It was the same as yesterday, and the day before. It was always the same, except sometimes they had eggs instead of cereal. There was no longer any bacon or ham as it had all been sold, except what had been crated for travel. The children knew better than to complain. The meal was finished in quick order, everyone following the pace of their mother, no muss and no fuss. There was always work to do.

Florence and Janie returned to the packing upstairs, and Janie started to cry. "Why do we have to leave our home? This is our house, isn't it?"

Florence stopped folding the huge, heavy quilt and sat on the side of their big cast iron bed with a loud sigh. "Yes, this is really our home and some day we'll get it back."

She hadn't noticed Jimmy-Dee standing in the doorway listening. Her brother was so young. Still he asked: "How come John R. thinks he owns our house?"

Florence was filled with sadness as she tried to find the words to explain to her younger siblings, "Now, now. You two come over here and sit by me on the bed and you'll feel better. Here now, let me tuck you into this big old quilt and warm you up." And as she did so the memories came flooding back from the time she and her mamma sewed this very quilt.

They had saved old pieces of dresses and coats and leggings, and even managed to salvage some of the heavy material from grandfather's old blue serge. That was three years ago and she had been just twelve as she watched Katie Ann's skilled hands take the tiniest stitches. Oh, what a feat that had been, making her first quilt. Florence loved the whole thing, especially taking apart the old coats and pants and other things, filling up the kitchen table in the evenings with scraps and pieces of mostly brown, black and grey remnants. And they even managed to find an old green wool jumper up in the attic. Mamma had thought it belonged to some old woman down in the glen. Anyway, the green was great because it brightened up the whole thing when they laid it down next to the small dark pieces of red flannel from Papa's underwear.

For days and days that winter the wooden quilt frame had stood in the kitchen making it difficult to cook and eat or do anything else. The quilt frame was made from spruce wood, from the trees up on the hill. It was old but still very sturdy. Florence's grandfather had made it for her grandmother, so many years earlier. She remembered Katie Ann telling her how it was made. It was special because grandfather had smoothed the wood for hours and hours, making sure there were no splinters sticking out here and there, and it had strong wooden dowels holding the arms together.

She laid down next to the youngsters and put her arm across their bodies as she began to tell Janie and Jimmy-Dee the sad story of why they had to leave home in the middle of the winter.

"You know John R. is our step-brother don't you?" She felt them nod their heads and decided she'd better be very brief and not make things too complicated for them to understand. "So, that means he is Papa's son. Papa had another wife who was John R.'s mother. Her name was Mary. She went to heaven when her baby boy, John R., was very little. So, many years later, when John R. was seven years old, Papa married our mamma, Katie Ann. So, John R. is not our real brother, only our stepbrother. You see, he is not our mamma's boy."

Jimmy-Dee began to squirm. Janie didn't make a peep, she just loved stories. So Florence continued: "I know you don't know John R. very well because he left Egypt when you two were very young – over five years ago. Janie, you were just one then, and Jimmy-Dee, you were only two."

By now Jimmy-Dee was getting out from under the warm quilt. "Anyway, you know when Papa went to heaven just this September, Mamma had a big shock."

"Why? Why was she shocked? She knew Papa was very sick for a long time," mumbled Jimmy-Dee.

"No, no, it wasn't the shock of Papa leaving this world. It was the shock of what it said in his last will and testament."

"What's a testament?" asked Janie.

"It's a piece of paper that tells everyone still alive what the dead person wants to happen with everything he used to own."

"So, what did Papa's last piece of paper say, anyway?" asked Jimmy-Dee.

"It said Papa wanted his son, John R., to have everything he owned, and our mamma was to get the horse and wagon and old Bessie, our cow."

The young ones were silent for a long time and then Janie screamed, "How come us and our mamma still can't stay in our home? How come?"

"Och, you're just too little to understand it all," whispered Florence. She still had her arm around her brother, hoping to keep him under the quilt for a while longer.

"How come John R. won't let us stay in our house?" asked Jimmy-Dee.

"I remember Mamma saying, way before Papa went to heaven, for us not to worry about things. We would be fine here on the farm. That we had everything we needed; that her own dear father made sure of that," continued Florence.

"What happened? How come Mamma told us if it wasn't true?" pouted the young boy.

"Oh, when you get older, you'll know better how things don't always work out the way we expect," said Florence, now folding up the quilt. She knew there was no point in telling the little ones any more of the story.

Katie Ann was having similar thoughts concerning the wording of both her father's and her husband's will. Bit by bit she was coming to grips with the harsh reality of her destitute circumstances. When Seamus, her father, had said he'd leave everything to her, he meant it. However, he couldn't have been thinking of the law and how it would all play out. Nor did he ever imagine his son-in-law would do what he did. It took everything she had to try and accept what had really taken place. Even though she knew when she married Alexander Gillis that the law said a husband owns all the assets of his wife, and such property becomes his on their wedding day, it had never entered her mind that Alec Beck would do what he did.

Katie Ann busied herself with emptying cupboards of bottles and cans, trying to sort out the old pantry. Her mind drifted off to past memories, memories of old stories told her over the years.

Alec Beck, her husband, a man of short stature – actually a tad shorter than Katie Ann – had been a strong man, thick in build from logging over the years. He was thirty-six years old when they married and brandished a fine black mustache and sparkling brown eyes. Some said he was a looker. He spent many of his nights swinging to the jigs and reels of the much-loved Scottish fiddles.

It was common practice to gather for a kitchen party. It didn't matter in whose house it was; the fiddles came out and the moonshine passed from mouth to mouth. People used to remark that Alec Beck could play the bones like no other in the area. "The bones" were actually two large spoons placed between the fingers to tap a beat onto the side of the leg. He was quite the catch as far as a fun-loving party bloke was concerned. When times were good, Alec Beck could always be counted on to pull a flask of rum from under his coat.

He had been one of the Gillis clan from down Gillisdale way. At the time they married, Alec Beck was certainly among the least-sought-after single men in the area. That was several years after his first wife had died in childbirth, leaving behind their son, John R.

In 1905, Alec Beck had led everyone to believe he was tired of his womanizing, a practice that had stretched from Maine to Inverness. He approached Seamus MacDonnell to inquire about Seamus' youngest daughter, Katie Ann. But Alec Beck had his eye on more than a new wife.

When it came to his real intentions, he wasn't as sincere or devil-may-care as he would have people believe. Under his flashy and debonair façade was a man on a mission. Alec Beck knew his son, John R, was growing older and needed more stability than he himself could give, especially after the boy's mother had caught consumption and died so suddenly. Alec Beck's own dear mother had passed away two years earlier, and he found himself with the burden of caring for his child.

No, as much as he boasted about his son and how much he loved him, Alec Beck was known to spew off about raising children being woman's work. So he wanted a woman. All of his relatives had enough of their own to feed and clothe; and besides, he also needed a place to hang his hat when the logging was done each fall. The Cape Breton winters were damn cold for a man not to have a real home of his own. His father had done what fathers before had always done, given the old Gillis property to his eldest son, Alec Beck's brother Rory Dan. So it was definitely time for him and his son to find a good place to live.

On a dark, cloudy afternoon, Alec Beck hitched a ride up the mountain, and on that ride he joked with his buddy: "Pretty soon, b'y, I'll have her made." As he jumped from the wagon, he knew he'd find Seamus MacDonnell tending his animals in the barn, and he turned and whispered, "With some luck I'll have a promise of marriage by nightfall." He was that kind of braggart. Even though he was still hung over, he certainly wasn't drunk, and with his head held high, proud like all the Gillises thereabouts, he entered the barn.

Seamus MacDonnell was getting on in years, and over time his own sons had become estranged from him. He had been strict with them, always expecting more. Times were harsh when they were growing up, and Seamus knew he stood to lose all he'd worked for if his sons couldn't show respect and responsibility for his wishes. He sometimes wondered whether he had actually driven them away. He never admitted to such; it was a ridiculous thought to blame himself. After all, he was certainly convinced that everything he did was for the good of his family. Some in the family might testify to a different story, that Seamus MacDonnell was full of himself, always keeping his eye on the goal. His goal was to have the biggest and most prosperous spread in the whole of Inverness County. And he did. He aimed to keep on building it until he died. More and more he wished he had developed a better relationship with his sons, at least one that was half as good as his relationship with Katie Ann.

Katie Ann remembered her father telling her how much he worried about her always taking care of him, having no life of her own; of how proud he was of her and how she had too much responsibility. She felt they held a mutual respect for each other.

Seamus knew, as soon as Alec Beck appeared that day, something unpleasant was about to occur.

As he stacked bales of hay on the August afternoon, Seamus' mind wandered back to the day a few months ago when he had taken the horse and buggy to town. He was ready to make the final decisions about his property. He remembered how disappointed Katie Ann was when he didn't ask her to come along. He just couldn't have her beside him that day. Seamus needed to think about things and didn't want any distractions. A long visit with his lawyer ended in his last will and testament being signed, sealed and delivered to the court offices. He'd explained it all to Katie Ann when he got back home. Seamus needed her to understand that her own future was secure.

Having completed this task should have brought him much relief and peace of mind but no, that wasn't so. The fact of the matter was he hadn't been feeling well lately. He'd developed a shortness of breath and he knew his age was against him. Pretty soon he'd have to stop all the heavy lifting and dragging.

So his mind had gone to his daughter and what would become of her, still single and all. And folks roundabouts didn't take kind to her. He knew that men shied away from her because she was half Micmac; to his shame, they even called her a squaw behind her back. He wished she had gone to Boston with her sister three years ago, but she didn't want to leave him. He felt bad about that, but still he loved her for it.

It had been years since either of Seamus' sons had come for a visit. Not because they were very far away: Hughie was only up in Port Hood, married to Maggie Taylor and already with two sons of his own. And Donald, Seamus' youngest, lived in the city. He had taken up with a widow in Sydney and got himself a job with a pick and shovel, working for the city. Donald thought himself a big man around town and wasn't at all interested in coming back to the farm, the home on Egypt Mountain—no way. However, Seamus knew in his heart that he had done the right thing by each of his children.

This was what he was thinking as his visitor entered the barn. So preoccupied was he with all these thoughts that the shadow of Alec Beck in the doorway kind of startled him and he found himself a bit jittery. Still he gathered his wits about him; on this particular day he knew without a doubt why this man was standing before him. Alec Beck Gillis wanted to marry his Katie Ann.

Ios, Ios, what am I going to do? He thought as he reached his hand out to Alec Beck in welcome.

"How'sha doin'," came the harsh-sounding voice. Alec Beck's tone had a way of grating on fellows' nerves.

"Fine, 'n you?" returned Seamus.

"Could be worse, ya know, but pretty good. I sees you're getting in the hay. The loft's nearly full. Looks good, it do."

Seamus took off his big gloves and laid the pitchfork against the post as he pulled up the stool for Alec Beck to take a seat. He slipped his hand under the old bench along the wall, reaching in to retrieve a flask full of golden brown liquid. "Will you join me in a drop?" he asked and handed over the opened jug.

Alec Beck took a long swig. As he passed the bottle back

to Seamus, he thought, *It's so good to taste such a fine whiskey.*

Seamus took a sip, put it down on the bench beside him then asked, "What brings you up the mountain this day?"

"Well, I can see you don't beat around the bush, Seamus, so I'll come straight to what's my intention."

Seamus saw the sweat gathering on the man's forehead and knew Alec Beck was not as confident as he pretended to be. He waited and didn't offer another drink.

"It's time I had me a new wife. My boy's getting older and needs a woman's touch, and besides I'm up in Maine more than half the year. And now that Mamma is gone, it's harder to care for him."

"I see," Seamus answered quietly.

Alec Beck didn't look happy and tried to keep his voice normal. "Can't you see what I'm asking, Seamus? I'm here to inquire about Katie Ann, your youngest. I knows from around that she's still unhitched."

"Yes, Alec Beck, my Katie Ann's a single lass and I don't hear her complaining about that fact. She's a fine, good woman and seems content being just the way she is. She has never mentioned the idea of having a husband. No, never said a word about it to me."

"Well, by God, everyone knows she's twenty years old and nearly considered an old maid. It's not good for her."

"Maybe you're right, but it's not my decision to make, now is it? Like you just said, she's a woman now and can make up her own mind." Even as these words were uttered, Seamus knew the man before him was right. How could a woman ever take on this farm and the animals, not to mention the planting and all the rest of it, by herself? There are no other fellows stopping off to ask for her hand, though. *Ios, Muire Bhan. How I wish he was some other than Alec Beck standing before me.*

It hadn't taken much figuring on Katie Ann's part to grasp the reality of her circumstances. She was very aware of her father's ill health and knew she couldn't possibly carry on without a husband. She thought maybe it could work, what with Alec Beck away for months at a time. She convinced herself she could put up with the rest.

Two weeks after the marriage, Seamus MacDonnell passed away.

If only Papa hadn't died so suddenly. Of course, he would have made sure of things. Katie Ann stopped her work, standing in the same spot as minutes before, then spoke aloud: "Alec Beck had the ungodly nerve to give my family's home and property to his first-born son and leave me and my children homeless and penniless. Och, for sure, the likes of him had nothing of his own to give away, what with his drinking and carousing all these years."

And so it was on that frigid, clear morning that Katie Ann and her four young ones left Egypt Mountain. Her hands were stiff from the cold as she finished tying Bella, the old cow, to the back of the wagon. Her thoughts plagued her, blackened like chimney soot, they were. She stared at the animal and wanted to give her a clip.

John R, her stepson, had arrived from Sydney the night before and had few words for either her or his step-siblings. It wasn't that he was actually to blame for his father's decision, but Katie Ann suspected he was in agreement with it. He didn't even get up in the morning to say good-bye to them. What a windfall it was for him, and at such a young age, only twenty-two years and now the owner of the biggest farm and acreage in the whole of Inverness County.

"God damn, and he never as much as milked a cow on this place since he was ten years old," muttered a weary and tired Katie Ann. Yes, way back then he'd made it known that he wasn't interested in farm work. He was a shy young fellow, more attracted to the city and a job on the highway than any farm duties.

"Ios, how in the name of God will I be facing the relatives in Sydney, especially Mary Ann Clarke?" Katie Ann muttered.

"Mamma, you're just making things worse. It's freezing and we're all just sitting in the cold, waiting," yelled Florence.

"Yes, yes, I knows it's cold. I knows." Katie Ann grudgingly picked up the reins and gave them a powerful whip.

"We are all sad, Mamma, but it's exciting too," said Florence.

Florence was secretly glad they were getting off the mountain. She had her own plan: as soon as she could, she was getting out of Cape Breton. *It's the Boston States for me, that's for sure,* she thought.

"Mamma, tell us about the times you visited Sydney," she said, trying to calm her mother down.

Settling herself on the sheepskin tied to the seat, Katie Ann looked back over her shoulder to make sure Joe-Hee wasn't sitting next to his brother for the long trip ahead. It'd be too hard on the little fellow: his brother never let up on him, pick and pick and pick, often making him cry. She hoped Jimmy-Dee would toughen up some when he made some new friends, but right now she was so grateful to Florence for keeping the boys occupied. Janie, the youngest, was tucked in beside Katie Ann.

She began to tell them about making this trip once before to the city in the winter.

"I was just turning thirteen then. My Papa had me bundled up so only my eyes were left bare for seeing. It was the time my brother Hughie got hurt and Papa went to see him in the old Salvation Army Hospital," said Katie Ann.

Florence had already forgotten she'd even asked her mother the question. Katie Ann continued: "Mamma didn't come. Mamma seldom came to the city. Some said she was too shy, but I knew that wasn't the only reason. It was more Mamma's shame. Shame kept her away from the gawking stares of strangers."

Florence realized anew how hurt her mother's feelings were. Katie Ann seldom mentioned her own mother.

Tears spilled over as Katie Ann stared for the last time at her childhood home. She thought a million thoughts in just a few seconds – too many memories, too much loss. *What's the use in lamenting? Things are what they are. I'll manage, all right, I will.*

So she struck out with her arm once again and the old horse took his first steps away from their home. The road leading down the mountain could have been worse but for the few folks from the village who had come up yesterday to bid them farewell. They had left a clearly defined trail in the snow making it less treacherous.

Ios, thanks to the Lord, no more snow fell overnight.

Katie Ann figured she'd land before nightfall if a storm didn't hit. It was five miles down the old Egypt Road into Inverness Town, where they would get onto Route 19, and another fifty-five miles from there to Sydney, then three more miles to the Clarke home. It was around five o'clock now. She'd been up since three this morning, securing the tarp over the wagon after it was loaded and doing last minute things - milking the cow, making sure the fire was low and the barn door shut tight, making a lunch of bread and old yellow cheese and some dried fish. The four of them had all helped, even Joe-Hee. He was jumping with joy about leaving the mountain and didn't care a darn about his mother's plight at all.

The wheels of her wagon were hitched underneath, tied on with heavy strips of leather, and from time to time they dragged in the drifts. They had been replaced with heavy wooden fir runners, six foot lengths of five-inch wide strips bent slightly upward in front and spliced underneath so they made deep ridges to prevent too much sliding. The sleigh itself was seven or eight feet long and four-and-a-half feet wide, with side panels three feet high, all made with the Douglas fir from their land. It was old and dusty but sturdy and had a million uses. Never had Katie Ann thought it would be used to move her and her family away from their home.

In case she had a problem on the way, Katie Ann planned to stick to the coast road, as it would be better travelled and safer. There were a good many animals in these woods, so best to avoid them as much as she could. For now, she was mighty careful as she guided the horse toward the top of the hill.

She could hear the rumbling of the water just beyond the bend, crashing down Egypt Falls. Her mind shot back to how grand and loud and scary it had been for her and her two sisters when they played games under the falls. She could still see them hiding on the rocky shelf just behind the roaring water. *Oh! What great times they were back then. Even this year my own kids did the same thing.* At this vivid picture a smile almost broke through.

"Oh! Yer telling the lieths again," came Jimmy-Dee's lispy voice from behind. And then she heard giggles from Florence, fooling him with a story about the ghosts hiding behind every tree. He was so scared he clung to her arm. Of course that didn't stop her. Katie Ann could hear her daughter spinning the folk tale about the old woman who disappeared fifty years ago. She was never found and some said she lurked in these hills, scaring the drawers off folks who happened to invade her territory. Katie Ann herself had no time for such foolishness.

Despite the fact of the road being only a few feet wider than the sleigh, they got onto the main roadway without mishap, and Florence said, "Mama, now it'll be a bit easier. Don't worry – we're doing good back here."

The roads had been opened up enough to allow the loggers to get their trees to the mills in Port Hawkesbury. Off the main road there were several inroads leading to the different coal mines.

Now for the third time today she started the rosary beads. Although her family had suffered many hard days in their lives, Katie Ann had never before been poverty-stricken. So again, on this dreary day, she couldn't seem to stop herself moaning. "How in the name of God, am I ever going to survive?"

She automatically removed her heavy mitten and shoved her right hand inside her coat to feel for the bulge against her undershirt, next to her breast. "Ios, Ios. Thanks Papa, for that blessed old habit of yours," she whispered to herself. "Always keeping a bit put aside for bad times. And what a blessing for

69

me that I never told old Alec Beck about the hole in the pantry behind the flour barrel. This'll do us until we gets on our feet, if I watches every cent, and I will."

"Mama, are you saying something to me?" came the muffled voice of the little one crouched beside her.

They made only four stops at the homes of relatives along the way. They knew pretty well everyone along the route, and everyone knew Katie Ann's circumstance and were sympathetic. Katie Ann had to fight back her embarrassment over what she knew folks were thinking. Still, they had to warm up and have a drop of tea and go to use the outhouse, so she hid her feelings as best she could. After all, it wasn't anyone's fault what was happening. Still, she was burdened with the heavy weight of her resentment, especially when they landed at Rory's door.

Alec Beck's nephew lived near the Seal Island Bridge. He and his wife had a nice spread just on the hill above the Bras d'Or Lake, giving them a spectacular view of the surrounding landscape. He was a fine gentleman himself and gave them a hearty meal of salty beef stew and biscuits when they gathered round the big kitchen table.

As hungry as she was, Katie Ann found it difficult to swallow her food; the lump in her throat almost choked her. She figured her pride had suffered enough that day to last a lifetime. "Stop, stop," she said to herself, "Stop all this weakness. You're thinking like a wretch, like it's the end of your life, or something." She turned to Rory's wife, Ethel: "This is the best tea I tasted in a long while. I thank you, indeed."

Back on the wagon, it seemed the longest day of Katie Ann's life as her thoughts drifted off to old memories of days gone by, days filled with hard work and contentment. She had actually been to Sydney at least ten times in her thirty-six years, twice as a child and other times for weddings or funerals. She had traveled with cousins and uncles, three or four wagons together, making sure there was a group ample enough to represent the Margaree and Gillisdale community during the mourning times. This time she was mourning her own passing, for it really felt as though part of her had died back there on the farm.

Coming into Sydney River, she brought the wagon slowly to a halt just to take a few minutes rest. It was coming on dark and the children were restless and hungry. She was nearly at Whitney Pier, where the Clarkes lived. She guessed she'd been on the road ten hours by now. Ordinarily, in the good weather of summer, it would have taken five hours or so to make the trip, but in the winter snow and ice it took twice as long. She just couldn't afford to take overnight lodging.

Ios, Ios, I hopes Archie got the message to my cousin, Mary Ann, about me and my brood's arrival this night. No one was about on Victoria Road, the main road of the Pier area. She took the left onto Mercer Lane and cursed the higher drifts of snow. Ten minutes later she pulled into the yard on Manse Street at the bottom of Mercer. Tears spilled once again, as Linus Clarke came from inside the barn and hugged her in the warmest of greetings then proceeded to unhitch Bella who was dropping on her feet, in need of milking. The kitchen door of the main house flung open and the vision of Mary Ann, whose girth practically filled the doorway, almost brought Katie Ann to her knees in a mixture of gratitude and humiliation.

STEAK NIGHT

Susan sat on the sofa in front of the television, not really watching anything in particular. She was totally beside herself with anxiety. After what happened yesterday, she swore she'd not be able to show her face in the Co-op grocery store ever again.

"God damn, anyway! What a mess Randy made of everything," she stammered, as she banged her fist down on the armrest beside her. She thought for the tenth time of the whole episode and knew she could not go on living this way. The whole thing began on Thursday afternoon when Susan announced she was going to get some groceries. Randy, her husband, started putting on his heavy raincoat, expecting to tag along, as he put it. Susan, as usual, was quite apprehensive about Randy tagging along. She thought to herself, *My Christ, why can't I ever get a moment's peace in my life? A woman can't even go do a little shopping by herself anymore.*

Susan's patience was wearing mighty thin, for the truth of it was that Randy was kind of light-fingered. There was no telling what he'd do in the store. It was always on Susan's mind: the shame of it nearly killed her, never knowing, when they went shopping together, what the hell would happen next. And of course this Thursday's episode took the cake. Her fear and embarrassment were over the top. Susan should have listened to her intuition and not ventured out at all. Her plan was to go by herself, take a stroll on the boardwalk, and have a Mocha Cappuccino before she picked up her groceries. "Of course," she muttered, "he'd have to spoil the whole plan."

Susan did go shopping and Randy did tag along. There was no pleasure in it at all because all the while she was in the store she had to keep her eye on him. At one point she saw the manager talking to Randy and her heart sank to her toes. She held her breath as she peeked through the pickle aisle at the two men talking. A crazy thought came into her head, a vision of Randy being arrested for shoplifting with his hands in manacles. She jolted back to the present when all of a sudden Randy spotted her and waved. *Thank God,* Susan thought: for sure Randy wouldn't be up to no good right in front of the manager.

She tried to relax a little as she stopped to chat with her friend Bonnie, and they actually had a little laugh together. Bonnie was always making fun, and today was no different. She told Susan about her son, Bob, getting caught necking with his girlfriend. They were parked down around the point. The police pulled up and shone the big light on them. "Shit," Bonnie said. "It's a good thing they still had their clothes on, or half on, anyway. Lord!"

Susan was at the cashier's counter, getting the groceries rung in and still scanning the store for Randy. Where the hell was he anyway? She sweated her way through the check out and practically stumbled out into the parking lot. There she spotted Randy standing by their car, clutching onto his coat. She knew something was up when he didn't help her put the stuff in the trunk and kept telling her to hurry up. On the way home, Randy kept his eye on the traffic, like he was watching for someone. Randy's mood changed from irritation to joking around as they neared their house. A few minutes later, standing in the middle of the kitchen, with his big trench coat hanging open, Susan's jaw fell to her chest.

"What are you up to now?" she asked.

"Oh, nothing much … except, I was wondering if you'd like to have a barbecue for supper?" said Randy, in a sneaky way.

All the bells and whistles went off inside Susan. "What, pray tell, are you thinking of barbecuing?"

"You'll soon see, girl. I picked up a few packages of meat," Randy said, as he pulled out the bloody packages.

"Meat? What kind of meat? I thought you said you were broke! When I mentioned getting a movie, you said you only had a few bucks to go to the tavern," demanded Susan, banging the cereal box down on the counter. By then Susan had a pain in her stomach. *Oh Lord!* she thought: *Not another anxiety attack coming on.* She sat down at the kitchen table trying to calm herself.

Just then Nicky, their ten-year-old son, came in the back door, yelling, "What's for supper? I'm starving."

Susan waited until she heard the door to Nicky's room close and the noise of his rumbling TV echoing into the hallway. Randy stood there, struggling to keep his laughter in, so the boy wouldn't catch on. He had the biggest grin on his face as he held the three packets under Susan's nose. "Now, by God, aren't these babies the most superb rib steaks you ever laid your peepers on? Yessiree, Bob, we are going to eat good tonight!" he bellowed.

Susan started to shake. This isn't the first time Randy has stolen food from the Co-op. *Why, in the name of Jesus, does he have to be a stealer?* she asked herself for the hundredth time.

"Randy, it's not like we can't afford steak, once in a while, anyway." She could hardly get her next words out of her mouth. "I told you the last time you did something like this, that if it happened again, I was leaving you. I don't want to live with a thief any longer. I mean it, Randy. If you don't get this stuff gone, out of this house immediately, I'm leaving."

Randy gathered up the packages and stuffed them back into his pockets. He was in some sour mood. "Man, why don't you just relax a little? Stop going ballistic. It's no big deal. If you don't want them, I'll take them to my sister Kay's. She'll definitely appreciate them. Her bunch of ruffians probably haven't seen a steak since God-knows-when." And with that, he stormed to the basement.

Shortly afterward, Susan heard the car starting up. "Thank God, he's getting that stolen meat out of our home." She had no appetite and definitely no desire to make supper. She'd order a pizza for Nicky and go take a long bath.

Randy hadn't returned home and it was getting onto 11:00 PM as Susan made her way down to the basement. She stood by the downstairs freezer, afraid to open it up. Of course she did open it and found the damn steaks. Pondering her dilemma, talking out loud to the freezer, she said, "What the heck am I going to do? I'd like to pitch them into the garbage, but what a waste. People are starving." She thought about her sister-in-law Kay and her kids, some of those same people. "Maybe I should just bring them to her house. It's a sin to throw them out."

After giving things more thought, Susan figured that there was only one hope for her and Randy to have peace and that was for him to return the meat to the store and apologize. To tell the manager he didn't know what came over him and say it was a joke or something. *We know the staff. That's the way it is in a co-op: everyone knows everyone.*

Randy was hung over until late Saturday afternoon and in no state to argue. "Of course," he admitted, to pacify Susan so she'd shut up, "It's wrong to steal and I shouldn't have taken the meat in the first place. I'll return the meat."

Susan wasn't sure what was worse, Randy stealing the meat or the thought of people knowing he did it. She was worried sick waiting for him to come back. It was taking a long time, indeed. Just as her imagination had gone berserk, visualizing Randy being arrested, charged, and doing time in prison, she heard their car pull into the driveway. She watched through the window as he skipped up the front steps.

Boy, that must have gone better than I thought it would. He actually looks happy, Susan said to herself.

"Hi, Babes. Want to go get a movie or something?" said the smiling Randy.

"Just a second ... what happened? What did the manager say? I was sick with worry," stammered Susan.

"I told you, girl, you worry too much for your own good. Everything's cool. It's all taken care of. Now, do you want to get a movie or not?" said Randy, with a sneer on his face.

"No, I don't want a movie. I want to hear what went on. Now!!" screamed Susan.

"Look," Randy boomed. "It's simple. I returned the steaks to the Co-op, just like you said. I went to the cash and laid them down on the counter and here's what happened."

"The cashier said, 'Hi, Randy – something wrong with the steaks?' "

"I just told her the truth. I said, 'Yes, as a matter of fact, there is a problem and Susan insisted I return them. And furthermore, I have a customer service complaint to make.' "

" 'What's the complaint, Randy?' "

" 'Well, see those white stickers on the packages, the ones with the small print?' I asked her, pointing to the stickers."

" 'Yes,' the cashier muttered."

" 'Well, the print is so small I didn't pay any attention to it. So, when I got home I just popped them steaks into the freezer. Today, when I went to take them out for the barbecue, Susan noticed the stickers. She told me they were not supposed to go into the freezer. It was marked right there on the packages, Previously frozen. Everyone knows you can't eat beef that has been re-frozen. My complaint is that the stickers are too small for anyone to notice and they should definitely be made larger.'"

"She was okay with that and said, 'I'll certainly pass on your complaint to our manager. Now, is there anything else, Randy?' "

" 'Just one more thing,' I said: 'I want a refund. Can't expect my family to eat poison steaks, can you?' "

Susan's face fell, as Randy kept on with his tale. "I just strolled out the door of the Co-op, stuffing the $57.60 refund into the front pocket of my jeans. I'm pleased as all get out with myself."

Like an afterthought, he continued: "It's weird how naturally these ideas come to me, all of a sudden, like. It's not like I planned it or anything. No, really – it's all so easy. A fellow can't help it, can he?"

Susan was dumbfounded – absolutely speechless.

Randy, continued, "Now, that's all there is to tell. And if you're not satisfied, tough. I'm going for a beer."

Linda Szabados

Was born in Garden Bay, B.C. and has lived on the west coast of Vancouver Island, including two years on a light station. She currently lives with her husband, an avid sailor, in Pender Harbour on the Sunshine Coast. She is a mother and a grandmother and has retired from a forty-five year nursing career. Her writing goals are to complete a series of horse adventures, and a Hungarian family story.

Time and Tide

One

The sign *Lacombe House* stood stark and bold. In smaller lettering below it said *Children's Home.*

Sandy MacLeod drove his car up the long winding drive and Theresa Sorenson, sitting quietly in the back seat, felt the lump in her throat nearly choke her. Annie MacLeod offered to accompany her but Theresa said no.

"I could come in and help you," urged Annie. "It's such a big decision. Sandy can have a little nap, while he waits." At this second request, Theresa stepped out of the car and walked quickly to the door. A nun ushered her down a long hall and into the matron's office.

"Have you filled out an application?" The matron turned briskly to the business of placing a child. "Name please," she said without looking up. After Theresa replied with her own and Abe's name, along with their marriage date, the matron went to her oak wall cabinet. In due course, she spoke with a kind tone.

"I have a letter here on file, a sponsor for your application. It seems to be from a Donald Yeats, M.D." The matron turned back to the desk and took up her pen, dipping the nib into the ink bottle and slowly drawing it across the bottle edge. She wrote silently for some moments, dipping her pen frequently. She turned the paper toward Theresa and said simply, "Sign please."

Carefully Theresa wrote her name; the matron then raised her blotter and placed it firmly over the document. She went to the door and rang a hand bell.

"Come along. Sister Martha will help you," the matron beckoned. As Theresa reached the door, she heard her deal sharply with Sister Martha.

"Tuck your hair in. I've spoken to you about this before. Now go to the mirror in my office at once." The matron and Sister Martha left Theresa standing in the hallway as the door closed behind them.

When the door reopened, Sister Martha hurried out and paused only long enough to beckon Theresa to follow. They entered a large room through thick double doors. The odor and crowding was oppressive: cribs lined the walls and little tables stood in the centre of the room amid intermittent noise and crying. As they walked forward, older children stared silently from their seats around the tables. Theresa stopped beside Sister Martha when she paused to speak to the other sisters bottle-feeding several babies. While she waited, Theresa's eyes focused and she looked around the room.

The beautiful brown eyes of the baby sitting at the far end of the room caught her attention. Their eyes met and held, so she went to him and sat down on the bare floor in front of him and held out her hands. He smiled and took one of her fingers in each of his. Her face glowed, responsively. He pulled himself up onto his knees, holding tight to her fingers. She took him into her arms and offered him the only toy she saw, a ragged, hatless, stuffed clown. He took it and offered it back to her; she laughed and he smiled. She knew it was love, sudden and unexpected.

"This is the one." Her confident words and strong voice caused the sisters to look up.

"He's a beautiful baby. We all love him." The response was enthusiastic. "He'll need a bottle of milk for the long trip home." Sister Martha went to a cupboard and filled a bag with clothes and diapers, and from the kitchen a bottle with milk. Finally Sister Martha wrapped the baby in a grey wool blanket donated by the Red Cross. Theresa turned to Sister Martha.

"Hold him for one minute. I'll be right back." Within seconds she returned, still smiling; in her hand the hatless clown.

While the sleeping baby rested in her arms, Theresa was vibrant and cheerful, talking and laughing on the return trip. Later Sandy MacLeod said to the men smoking on the porch of his general store: "I'd never give it credence, the change that came over that woman once the baby was in her arms. It was like the sun came out after a long rainy season."

At the same general store, Theresa proudly introduced her son, Barry, to the community. The subjects of colic and teething were discussed by the experts. Aunt Hattie Tremblay had advice and pride enough for all the women.

"It's like this," she said, spreading the flannelette diaper on the store cutting board. "You fold it like a kite." Her ample body swayed as she drew Theresa and the women around her with authority, deftly folding the square cloth into a fitted diaper. "Run the barb of the safety pin through your hair or a bar of soap. That way, it will run through the cloth smoothly," Hattie demonstrated.

Not long after the adoption, the priest made his way to the farm. Theresa recognized him in the distance, and as he drew nearer she felt only anger. The past action of the priest still burned in her mind. He had hurried to her father with the rumor that some of the girls on the baseball team were pregnant, and she had been forced into marriage at sixteen to Abe Sorenson, the fifty-year old farm hand. Unjustly sentenced, she had not forgiven the priest's interference. Since that day she had avoided the church and hadn't seen the priest.

"I see you've come a long way today, Father." Her tone was stern, her face unsmiling.

The priest sat on the porch step, out of breath.

"I've come to see about baptizing the baby," he spoke when his breathing steadied.

From the upper pasture, Abe had seen the approach of the priest, and he made his way with long strides towards them.

"I won't need to baptize the baby again. I'm sure the Sisters of Charity did it at the orphanage," Theresa spoke coldly.

"No, that's not the way it's done." The priest began

again, but was interrupted by Abe

"I'm Lutheran, so the baby will be taking my church." He spoke quietly, then turned toward his team of horses and looked at the priest. "I can give you a ride a ways into town now."

Theresa hurried into the house. She was afraid the priest would curse her with eternal damnation, and ashamed that she would deserve it for the great reservoir of resentment she harbored. Inside she picked up her sleeping Barry and cradled him, singing softly, and taking comfort from him. Stillness came to her.

Two

When Theresa saw the door close behind Barry and his bride-to-be, she grimaced and faced her sister, Marie. Anger was visible in the hard lines around her mouth and the deep grooves between her eyebrows. Marie glanced at Theresa and spoke quickly.

"You hate her, Terry. I can see it in your face," Marie accused her older sister. Shaken, Theresa turned away and started toward the living room of Marie's Edmonton bungalow, collecting dishes, ashtrays and other remnants of the bridal shower. Reviewing the evening, she justified her dislike of Barry's choice for a wife.

A trivial, self-absorbed young girl, Theresa thought. One who had never done any serious work in her life. What would Barry's life be like, and how would she be able to watch it? How would they all be able to live in her home together, even for a short time? The situation seemed intolerable. Theresa returned to the kitchen and went to the back porch in silence to empty the ashtrays.

Her mind travelled through the stages of Barry's childhood, adoring him. When she gained control of her voice, she spoke.

"I've been thinking of leaving," Theresa said with

hesitation, then continued sadly. "You know Barry's graduating in June, and getting married this summer. I'll just be in his way."

Marie turned from the sink. "A fine time to go," she replied. Since Abe's funeral, she had wondered when Theresa would break free.

"Yes, Terry. You must be forty-two this birthday. Lots of living to do yet. Where do you want to go?" Marie spoke brightly, keeping dismay out of her voice.

"I think I'll sell my old car, and take the bus to the coast. We loved Vancouver, didn't we?"

Marie only nodded.

During Barry's graduation ceremonies, Theresa's face was like a casting, hiding the range of emotions that flooded over her. Afterwards she visited her family to explain her plans. Her brothers expressed approval, but Marie became distant and detached.

Theresa was on the bus that left Edmonton before sunrise. Seated beside a window, she absorbed the beauty of farmland flat and rolling – horses in pastures, dogs in farmyards, familiar scenes. When the Rocky Mountains came into view, Theresa counted the Seven Sisters shoulder to shoulder. As the bus rounded a bend, more mountains appeared, continuous and interlocking, dusted with frosting near the peaks and fine chiseled tips, some flat glaciers with the sun glowing brilliantly in the early daybreak. Passing through the mountains, the foothills rolled into aqua lakes, water courses and forests. Later, contrasting with the evergreen forest, the sand-colored plateaus of desert extended to the horizon. As the hours passed, Theresa's head slumped back and she slept. The setting sun flashed glorious colours over the lush green fields of the Fraser Valley, and when she reached Vancouver, the lights sparkled and invited her back again after twenty-four years away. But the city traffic and noise no longer excited Theresa, and she took a bus to an up-coast village.

She stood on the wharf breathing the salt air, while seagulls screamed and circled on the wind currents above the harbor. *I'm home*, she thought, and a thrill of adventure caused her to shiver in the brisk wind. She stayed in a cold, musty motel while she took stock. In the local paper she scanned the classified ads for a place to rent.

At Bingo, the village came alive with casual friendships, an inroad to community life. She found a place to live just above the fishermen's wharf, a small suite partially furnished, its windows and doors opening onto the harbour. She put her name in at the fish plant, where she found summer work and combined it with a part-time shift at the local coffee shop. When the rain began in earnest, and the fish plant closed for winter, Theresa took an interest in a regular customer.

Joe had coffee every morning at the cafe near the government wharf. When Theresa poured his coffee the first time, she felt young, teenaged, and her hand shook; the coffee spilled and she laughed nervously.

His smile started slow, at the wrinkles around his brown eyes. Like a Chinook wind blowing in to unthaw the grip of winter, he brought her to life in a way she'd never known. Playing cribbage in the cozy cabin of his fish boat, walking hand in hand along the waterfront, eyes locked together in conversation, laughter over small things, all tokens of their gathering love. Unsought, love came to them.

It was while she washed the dinner dishes and wiped the table before folding it to make room for the bunk that he spoke casually with his head out the door, his words drifting on the breeze.

"Come fishing with me this summer. I need a deck hand." As he stepped out on deck, she swung her slight body in front of his and looked at him with hands on hips, blue jeans snug and cuffed at mid-calf. She wore a little cotton blouse with the collar turned up at the back, her torso tipped, breasts straining against the material.

"What kind of a question is that? You want a deck

hand and a worker, not a woman?" Joe looked down at her, bewildered, then suddenly took her face in his big rough hands and kissed her, long and hard. When he released her, he spoke softly.

"Of course I want you for my woman." As he spoke, he ran his hands down her arms, pulling her to him. "I think you'll make a fine deck hand too." He chuckled.

She leaned into him and quit her job the next day. With her last pay check she bought gumboots, rain slicker and pants.

In readiness for the fishing season, they shared the spring boat work. Their newfound love filled the burdensome tasks of painting and engine work with delight.

As she fried baloney for sandwiches, it surprised her that she took pleasure in everything. She located mustard from the small shelves behind the folding table and it sizzled on the hot baloney. When she handed him a sandwich and tea, Joe smiled the slow easy smile that caused Theresa's whole being to soften.

As the salmon opening neared, haste permeated all activities. After groceries were stowed, Theresa's thoughts turned to her son in Alberta.

In the pay phone at the top of the wharf, she dialed Barry. His voice over the line brought a smile to her face.

"Hi Mom. I got your letter – just hadn't found time to write back."

Quickly she cut in: "It's okay; I know how busy you are. Listen, Barry, I'm going fishing. I'll be away two months at least. I'll call you when I can. Oh, and tell Marie. Promise you'll phone her right away, and tell her? Oh, and that I've met someone."

Barry's voice came back to her and she could see him smiling. "Good for you, Mom. I hope he's good to you. I'll tell Marie."

Theresa put the phone back on the hook and smiled. She stepped out of the phone booth, breathed the sea air and felt like skipping.

Theresa and Joe stood together watching the sun sparkle

on the ocean, a thousand diamonds winking and shimmering. Clearing the harbor, the fishing vessel turned north and seabirds swam away, some diving quickly in sudden fear. Often dolphins would appear suddenly and play in the bow wave. A lone grey whale surfaced and silently slipped its barnacle-crusted body back into the depths. These treasures Theresa seized as Joe pointed them out to her.

Boat travel was long and time seemed to stand still. Scenery came into view and passed from sight so slowly that Theresa began cleaning. She gathered all the loose change from the shelf under the pilot house windows. Tossed pennies had turned green, and the coins had white mold from age and contact with sea water. She painstakingly cleaned and rolled the money, and Joe smiled at her diligence. Never had the boat been so clean

Up a long channel, they turned in to a wharf to take on fuel and fresh water. Joe was smiling as he tied the boat and chatted with a man on the gas dock. Suddenly he came back to the boat and seized Theresa's hand.

"Come on, this'll give you a chance to stretch your legs. I'll show you around." They walked hand in hand up the ramp, and Theresa's eyes widened as she took in the lawn leading up to a large, white clapboard building surrounded by flower beds.

"It's a hospital. The doctor comes from the prairies. This is what you call a mission hospital. Just maybe the doc will be around and we can get him to marry us." Joe smiled down at Theresa and lifted her off her feet with a hug.

The spontaneous request for a marriage was not unusual and the staff hurried to help make the day special. A nurse went to the garden and came back with a bouquet of red poppies and star-shaped white flowers on trailing vines. Theresa and Joe stood together and exchanged vows. Happiness was in their faces and the enthusiasm in the staff's congratulations cumulated with the cook throwing rice as they hurried back to the boat to catch the tide.

For many years the salmon were plentiful and the price good. Joe spent long hours standing in the stern bringing the fish aboard. Holding a cigarette between his teeth, squinting to avoid the smoke in his eyes, he smiled at Theresa while she stood on deck watching the fish. His mood was exuberant as he lifted her, squeezing her against his wet, fish-scaled coveralls. They laughed together.

Sometimes they sold to a cash buyer, and Joe always put the money into her hand like it was too hot to handle, as though it would burn him. She opened a bank account, paid income tax, and watched it grow. They paid cash for the little cottage facing the harbor and lived happy, fifteen good years. Such good years.

At the end of their last season, when all the work was done, Joe stumbled as he walked up the ramp. A box fell from his arms and he collapsed onto it. Theresa, cleaning the cabin, didn't look up until the ambulance siren got close. Someone was running to her, shouting her name, yelling that Joe had collapsed. She couldn't stop her screaming as she ran to him.

She went with Joe in the ambulance to the hospital. She watched, transfixed by fear, as attendants bent to the task of giving CPR; and while his body remained unresponsive, they transferred him into the emergency staff's care.

Theresa was directed to seating, where kind hands placed a coffee cup into hers. She placed it untouched on a table. Hospital staff walked by, their images blurred. She couldn't get air and her vision began to distort. Attempting to stand, her body refused and crumpled onto the hospital floor. A nurse helped her onto a bed and tried to explain Joe's sudden death.

Theresa's face became a mask of stone. The nurse stretched a cotton weave blanket over her, then left her in the empty day-care room. When she returned, Theresa was shaking, her eyes wide, mind numb and unable to respond to a simple question. She winced when the nurse administered a needle. She slept for a few hours then woke screaming Joe's name.

"Get out of the hospital – get outside! Fresh air will help,"

urged the voice in her head. She put on her socks and running shoes, then silently hurried past rooms and closed doors, down a back hallway and out the emergency doors. She swung her body into her jacket and hurried away from the hospital lights.

Instinctively she turned toward home, and the night air refreshed her. Joe's death became clear and real, stark in Theresa's thoughts, while her body felt cavernous.

Three

"How could you Joe? How could you leave me!" Theresa hissed into the cold night air. The helpless feeling of loss turned to anger, a surging anger flowing like lava.

"I needed you and you left me, just like her. Yes, just like her." Theresa walked fast, almost running. "I never told you my mother left us. Just up and left the farm, took the cows and walked off. She deserted us kids – me, Marie and the boys." She kept to the paved road, away from the village lights.

"How could you leave, Mother?" she spoke aloud, moving onto the pavement because the roadsides were soaked in dew and damp was seeping into her feet.

"I have never forgiven you. Never! Then there were the trees. All those trees I cut down and you promised me ten cents a tree. Why didn't you tell me the truth, that you couldn't or wouldn't pay me? A hundred trees – hard, hard work for a child! What were you thinking, Mother?"

Theresa looked closely at the near distance, checking her progress. It was cold, so she kept a brisk pace. Occasional house lights winked through trees and shrubs, then suddenly car lights. She stepped onto the grass and further into the trees, waiting while the car passed.

Theresa continued this time to herself: "You're strong – didn't it give you strength?" As she spoke, the memories flooded in. She saw herself as a twelve-year-old, keeping the children fed, looking after the farm by herself. Her father had worked in Edmonton, so he was away when their mother left. Every night Theresa made hot cocoa while they waited for their Father to come home. A tablespoon of cocoa, sugar and cream stirred briskly into each cup until thick foam rose to the top as she poured in hot water. She realized she had given strength to her family, and the longing for her mother had forged within her the qualities of motherhood.

She was climbing a long hill. At the crest she paused and through fir trees caught glimpses of the waves sparkling faintly in the light of a partial moon.

As she rounded a corner and came clear of the roadside bushes, the ocean roar filled the stillness. To the east a pale strip of light exposed the pounding surf. As she watched the wind blow the white foam and spray from the crest of the waves, she thought how God was like the ocean. She moved onto the beach and sat on a log.

This was her confessional, here on the beach in the middle of the night. Suddenly she was on her feet, walking to the surf and shouting as anger rose in her throat.

"And then there was Abe! Why did I have to marry him? How could my own father agree to the priest's idea! He said I was pregnant. Where did a lie like that come from? What did he know? My God, I just wanted to play baseball!"

She was a lone figure on the beach, hands on her hips shouting into the wind and sea. Her shouts mingled with man's garbage – shipwrecks, engines, skidders, cars – all sinking into the sand without a trace.

The team colors ... her uniform blouse and pants ... her home runs. Hitting the ball way out, seeing herself running, taking each base, and finally home plate. The cheering of her little brothers Paul and Luc jumping up and down, shouting her name. She was their hero. She saw their smiling faces and herself walking home with little Luc's hand in hers.

Then the visit from the priest, and it was over – baseball finished in mid-season. She remembered her father's anger. Days of accusatory raving followed by the marriage. Words said in a jumble with no one to hear her silent defense: that it was a lie; that she wasn't pregnant. Theresa felt her heart pounding like the ocean surf. She wrapped her arms around her thin body and cried.

As she sat back on the log, she turned her face to the pale light brightening the sky above the ocean. Her mind went back to Abe and she shuddered, thinking of the revulsion she had endured. No love, just the act; and she had run from it. She and Marie had gone to Vancouver and freedom.

Then a letter had come. "Abe is sick. He needs you, Theresa," wrote her brother. It was Paul's plea for family, and in it Theresa recognized his cry for the mother who had failed them. Then guilt filled her with remorse that she had chosen to leave like her mother. She went back to care for the husband she'd left.

Four

The bus had arrived at the Edmonton depot after a trip through the worst winter driving conditions. Passengers disembarked looking tired and untidy. Arriving from Vancouver, Marie and Theresa were not dressed for the painful cold. They grasped their suitcases and looked up and down the road.

"I hope they'll come and meet us," Theresa spoke irritably while Marie lit a cigarette. "I'd forgotten how cold it is," she muttered as she rubbed her arms. "And we have no money for a hotel."

As she paused, a mud-splattered truck moved erratically towards them, horn honking. It stopped beside them and smiles radiated the two sisters' faces.

"Well, well, you've made it home!" Their father's voice shouting with excitement, arms wide to embrace both daughters at once. Theresa and Marie kissed and hugged both father and brothers, then turned to hug their father a second time. Luc and Paul lifted the suitcases into the back of the truck.

"You look wonderful, truly you do. Now let's get home or you'll catch your death of cold, dressed so poorly." Their father's voice resonated with pride. They crowded into the cab and bounced over the frozen ruts on the road. Talk was loud above the noise of the engine, Paul and Luc telling of farm life, hunting, and community news.

A hush fell as their father maneuvered the truck along Abe's farm road and up the rise to the house.

Strange, thought Marie. *What can we say?*

Theresa noticed the sudden silence and spoke with assurance. "Well, we have to get this over with. It's why I came back." The truck pulled up beside the farmhouse and Paul helped Theresa down through the snow and into the house. He went with her into Abe's sick room. On an old worn sofa, Abe lay inert, perspiration visible in beads on his forehead.

"I've come to help you get well." Theresa's voice was thin and breathless.

Paul understood her discomfort. "You're in good hands now, Abe. Just lay back and rest." He spoke like his father, almost at a shout, loading firewood into the stove before he left the room. "We'll come and do farm chores in the morning."

Theresa waved from the porch then turned toward her loathsome task.

"Paul wrote, said you were sick and needed help. It was a long trip all the way from Vancouver. Have you had something to eat?" She didn't pause for Abe's reply, but left the room to fill the kettle. Abe turned his face towards the floor to hide the tears glistening in his eyes.

Theresa put the full kettle back on the stove and turned to evaluate the cupboards in the disorderly kitchen.

"Didn't Aunt Hattie come over and cook up a meal?" Theresa felt her temper rise and checked herself. As she put on Abe's boots and coat, she shouted back to him. "I'm going to the barn for eggs and potatoes."

In the dim light of the barn, she saw everything was the same. The hay was piled ceiling-high, the egg boxes were full of straw, and the potatoes were in the same place, cold but not frozen. The carrots were in sand.

Back in the kitchen, she found braided onions and cut one free to make a meal of potatoes, onion, and eggs. She placed his plate on an apple crate beside the sofa, and turned with the kettle to make tea. After searching the kitchen for his mug, she found it on the floor near the sofa, his old brown mug stained by a dark crack running up one side.

"Here it is. Now we both need tea." Theresa reached into the cupboard for a cup for herself and wondered if she could bear the silence. At the very back of the shelf she recognized the fine bone china cup and saucer, gold-rimmed with a spray of lilac, a gift from Abe.

Noting the dusky color of Abe's skin and the beads of perspiration, Theresa made plans. "I'm going to get the local doctor here as soon as he can come," she spoke with finality.

Over the customary cup of tea, Dr. Yeats gave Theresa instructions. She wrote them down and followed his orders. As Abe began to improve, the doctor wouldn't need to come again and now his mind turned to Theresa, a young woman with a very elderly husband on a lonely farm.

"I don't suppose you've heard of the Lacombe House down in Calgary?" Dr. Yeats bent his head to study the pattern on the oilcloth, and paused to consider his words. Clearing his throat, he raised his voice just slightly and continued. "It's an orphanage, takes in wee bairns, and poor unwanted children. It's run by the Sisters of Charity of Providence." Again he paused, gulped his tea and rose to complete the house call. "You'd give a young child a good home. It would be a fine thing!"

The doctor paused to accept his hat and coat from Theresa and turned his attention to Abe. "Now I'll be off. Keep that man from sudden work. Just build to it gradual." The doctor closed the door behind himself and Theresa remained standing near the stove. Abe spoke from his chair, without looking at Theresa.

"It'd be a good thing to give a young 'un a home. And we have plenty of food."

Five

The lights of the small rural hospital glittered in the November rain. Staff began arriving for the night shift while a female voice over the sound system ushered visitors out. Under the bright lights of the nursing station, staff gathered for Report. The charge nurse completing her shift began reading from the file.

"Theresa Ronson, age eighty-two. Patient of Dr. Klien, diagnosis COPD, CVA. She came in by ambulance this afternoon in poor condition. Color dusky, short of breath. She lives alone so may have been in this condition for some time and become dehydrated. Her family is out of province. She has an IV running slowly, oxygen at 4 liters, Ativan for restlessness, and Ventolin via nebulizer, Q.I.D."

Report completed, nurses began answering call lights. Others stocked the evening nourishment trolley while the team leader began her rounds. At Theresa's bedside the nurse stopped, fingers seeking a wrist pulse while her eyes scanned the IV site.

"Joe," Theresa mumbled. "Joe." Her voice trailed off, but her hand went out to grasp the bed rails and her leg struggled against the bed sheets.

"Theresa," the nurse spoke softly. "You're in hospital. Just rest and get stronger." As she adjusted the oxygen mask, she spoke again: "Theresa, my name is Lynn and I'm here to look after you tonight. I'm just going to leave now and get you some medicine."

As she left the room, the evening care trolley was being propelled down the hall by staff settling patients for the night. At this time the ward changed from the daytime bustle to a warmer and friendlier place where refreshments, backrubs and communication created a caring environment. It was here that nurses learned of patient's fears, difficulties, and sometimes their life stories. Theresa received mouth care and a back rub; the draw sheet was replaced, pulled tight and wrinkle free, and the pillows turned.

The charge nurse made a phone call to Barry Sorenson, Theresa's next-of-kin. Unanswered, she put the receiver down.

"Call again in the morning just before Report," she concluded. At 6:00 AM she dialed again. The phone rang in Sorenson's Alberta home.

"Hello? Yes, this is Barry Sorenson." He paused while the nurse told him of his mother's condition. "Will she be okay?"

"Your mother has had a stroke," was all he heard.

"Can you call me tonight? Maybe she'll improve."

Barry turned from hanging up the phone, and went into the bedroom to see if Connie was awake.

"Connie, that was about Mom. She's in hospital – she's had a stroke. The nurse said her condition is very serious." Connie sat upright, swung her legs out of bed and spoke without looking at her husband.

"You know how busy we are right now. The end of November has all the Christmas functions, and this weekend is the Eastern Star dinner and dance fundraiser. You've got to be there."

Barry nodded, and his mind turned to his work schedule. "I've got that important conference in Calgary on Monday too. I'll keep in touch with the hospital. Maybe she'll come out of it." He put on his jacket and straightened his tie.

For the remainder of the week, anxiety robbed Barry of long periods throughout his days; in between life resumed its rhythm. He phoned the hospital daily and on the weekend called his Aunt Marie and Uncle Paul and Luc. After his Monday meetings in Calgary, Tuesday was spent in follow-up, working late into the evening. Falling exhausted into bed, he slept soundly.

He awoke startled from his dream. He and his mom had been playing catch, and he remembered her running backward, her golden brown hair bouncing as she backed up to catch the pop fly. Her arm was reaching, baseball glove high over her head.

It was his mom, calling his name that woke him. In the darkness, he got out of bed and went into the kitchen and made coffee. He thought of her love for the game, and their pride when the baseball gloves—one for each of them—had arrived from the catalogue order. Suddenly he made plans to go to her right away.

He showered, went into the bedroom, and turned his bedside light on. Connie stirred and mumbled.

"What time is it?"

Barry quickly filled his overnight bag. "Early. I'm going to fly out to see Mom."

Connie sat up. "Why don't you wait till the weekend? Then Jenny can go with you. She hasn't been to the coast in years."

Barry straightened and spoke angrily. "Dammit, Connie. It's not a sightseeing trip … it's about my mother! I'm getting an early flight, even stand-by will do. I'll call you tonight."

Rain beat against the ferry windows; the sky was low, cutting the view of the coast mountains. Barry searched through the newspaper for the sports page, but nothing caught his attention. He put the paper aside, unread, and turned his face to the sea.

Throughout the week the nurses had discussed Theresa's failing condition, speculating her death would be anytime. By midweek her intravenous fluids and breathing medications had been discontinued. Now she was supported by comfort measures.

As the days passed, some nurses wondered what was holding Theresa. During Report someone interrupted.

"She has a son. Maybe she's waiting to say goodbye. She may need to see him … even just feel him near."

The charge nurse had tried phoning Barry again, but again failed to reach him.

Theresa's breathing became slow with delayed pauses

of suspended breath, yet she continued. The nurses talked out their concerns as they sat in their lounge on a break.

"She's a lapsed Catholic. One of her friends came in on Sunday and mentioned that something had turned her away."

The charge nurse looked up sharply, stared thoughtfully at the nurse speaking, then went to her desk to call Sister Mary Margaret.

When the nun reached the ward, the charge nurse was waiting to direct her to Theresa's room. Sister Mary Margaret bent near Theresa's ear to speak the familiar words and placed the rosary into her hand.

She began the Lord's Prayer slowly, her voice clear, and then her memory took her unfalteringly into the Apostles' Creed, and finally the Rosary.

When Sister Mary Margaret completed her mission, Theresa's erratic breathing changed to a deep quiet sigh. It hung suspended.

The charge nurse entered the room placed her fingers on Theresa's wrist. "She's gone."

Sister Mary Margaret and the nurse stood in silent respect for the passing. The room was still with relief.

As Barry Sorenson entered the hospital he felt a wave of nausea. Directed by admitting to the ward, he was given date and time of death, and the nurse at the desk passed him a shopping bag containing his mother's effects. He left the hospital and hurried through the heavy rain to his rental car.

He drove to the cottage on Harbour Lane, where he paused, noting the locked door.

The key was under the mat. It turned in the lock and the door swung wide, opening into the living room. Clearing the threshold, he stood like an intruder.

His eyes scanned photos of himself at all ages – on horses, in baseball uniform, on his grandfather's shoulders and with his father, Abe, on the wagon seat.

And then, on the shelf among the photographs, he saw

his mother's soft calf-hide baseball glove, a baseball cradled within it. He took it into his hand, and as he turned it he saw his mother's writing: "Barry's first home run, July 1955."

Frank MacKenzie

Is a retired teacher. He grew up on the Sunshine Coast then left for a teaching job, but has recently returned to the coast, only to linger around local coffee shops. Wanting to use his time more productively, he decided to try writing.

Fireside

I don't remember
anymore
except
for random images,
embers of memories
glowing,
rising on invisible agitated currents,
drifting into blackness.
Sparks of the past
waken dream fragments
of hazy, smouldering
glimpses
singed in time.

Unchained

I came to find liberation
to drive the shovel forcefully into the loam
repeatedly turning the clumpy rooted sod
to expose the dormant shoot
withered by temperate winter freezes and thaws
moulding in my narcissistic introspection

In my laden imagination
the shoot becomes a strangling vine
on a hewn lattice frame
Fermented berries
blur my ponderous thoughts
like gorged pollen dust
sinking beneath the water`s surface
caught in the swirled time flow
of dream fragments
making ungraspable
the stark awareness
- of self.

The Assist

In his twenties, Darrell worked hard when he could find work. He and his mates were enjoying an evening at the pub.

Darrell raised his beer mug and took a long sip. It tasted good.

Rob, sitting across from Darrell, spotted a weathered man entering the pub. "It's Trig Bjornson and I bet he's looking for a deck hand."

The man stooped slightly as he walked, scanning the pub. Bjornson's face was tanned and he had wrinkles around sepulchral eyes. He approached Darrell's table. "You seen my regular hand?"

"Nope. He's probably getting drunk down at the Legion. Hard getting a deck hand on a Saturday night." replied Rob.

"Sure is," Trig agreed in a weary voice. He wore a toque, a shabby green coat, and loose bulky pants. His face bore his thirty-eight years of running tugs. "Any of you interested in coming out for six to ten hours?"

"What doing?" Darrell asked. He felt the need to line his pockets.

"An assist," Trig replied. "Helping the *Harmac Cedar* tow a boom across the strait. Twenty bucks an hour."

Darrell would miss his Saturday night beers, the chance to meet a woman – but money was money. "I'll go."

"Drink up. Truck's outside"

At the government wharf, Darrell followed Trig down the incline to the floats and walked over to the *Stormer*. It was a steel-hulled tug, decades old, sunk once, with a rebuilt wheel cabin.

He boarded the craft. Trig opened a hatch and descended down a ladder into the engine room. Darrell remained above deck; he saw no need to follow. He could see the view of the wharf, the harbour, and the quaint sprawling village. It was almost twilight.

Darrell noticed a large fir tree on the bottom slope of the nearby rock bluff. He heard the raucous cawing of many crows. Then the tree became silent: a single crow flew out. Several seconds later, twenty to thirty followed the same flight path taken by the first bird. A pursuit was underway. The cawing recommenced. The clamouring rose and fell, then built to a crescendo. Once again silence; then another bird flew out. Over a score of birds followed the single crow.

Fascinated by the tree, he didn't notice when Trig reappeared from below.

"There's something happening in that fir tree," Darrell said, pointing.

Trig focused on the tree. He tuned into the harsh cawing which had resumed. "Looks like a crow court. Seen them before"

"What the hell is a crow court?"

"Those damn black things – those killers of smaller birds – they have a social code. All that squawking is their way of communicating."

"You're putting me on," Darrell scoffed.

"I ain't. They're deciding the fate of those who have broken crow law."

Silence descended again. After a delay, the ritual of one crow followed by tens of others was repeated. "See that crow flying solo?" Trig explained. "It's condemned. The other birds will cut it down and peck it to death."

"How do you know?"

"Just do. Seen it a hundred times."

"Harsh punishment," Darrell added.

"Crows are thieves and scavengers, but they have their taboos. Like people, some always break'em."

"What the hell could a crow do to get condemned?"

"Stealing eggs, eating the young, breaking territorial rights – that sort of thing. Could even latch on to another's mate," Trig said with a hint of a chuckle.

"Bloody intelligent and cheeky," said Darrell, beginning to believe in the idea of crow courts.

"You know," the skipper started, "there's a rookery behind my place. Maybe hundreds of crows call it home at night."

"The racket must bug you."

"No. I've a feel for crows. We've a rapport, you might say. Me and crows, we're both creatures…" Trig stopped, realizing that valuable time was being wasted. "Can't stand around talking. Go cast off the stern line."

The skipper put the diesel into reverse and the *Stormer* backed into the harbour. He pushed the gear control forward and the steel tug responded. He held back on the throttle due to incoming boat traffic and the desire to avoid making a large wake.

The *Stormer* ploughed out the harbour gap and into the open strait. Bluffs, beaches, and wooded shoreline, now shrouded in dusk's shadows, fell behind. Trig poured some water into a battered coffee pot, set it on a small stove then returned to the wheel and watched for deadheads or logs. The tug rode to and fro in the open water. Darrell sensed the motion and the beers he'd drunk earlier.

The two men rambled on in conversation. They talked about tugs that had sunk, usually dragged down by a barge in tow during a storm. They talked about civil servants enforcing bureaucratic regulations that had provoked Trig into many a shouting match. Chuck Hanson, owner of the *Dauntless* became the focus of their conversation.

"Larsen and me had one hell of a go the other night. Almost came to blows," the skip recalled.

"What over?"

"Log bundles. I towed them over to the L&K booming grounds, put them right where I was supposed to. They were low in the water. Larsen couldn't find them. He only had to look harder. He was sure that I had towed them over to the Fraser's north arm."

"The arse."

"Larsen was pissed off – no reasoning with him," the skipper continued. "He's a cutting bastard. He thinks I'm crooked and strange because I keep to myself. Finds it unnatural that I know so much about birds – 'specially crows.

The look in Trig's eyes grew distant. Darrell saw it for what it was. People who shunned others often had that gaze.

" I can mimic birds. Even talk to them," said Trig.

There was a long silence. Darrell began to feel uneasy. "How long you been working this tug?" he asked to fill the gap.

"Fifteen years. But I've been on the sea since I was a kid. I work hard and get the job done. Yeah, tug boating's hard work – can't go on forever."

Trig peered through the window in front of the wheel. He kept course by pointing the *Stormer* towards a distant beacon that was becoming more visible as darkness fell.

Below, the engine din was pervasive. The prop generated a frothy, powerful wake which could be seen out the rear of the cabin. Trig could just make out high overcast, portending rain and gusts. "Weather could go either way. Bit of a south easterly coming up," he surmised. "The *Harmac Cedar* is anxious to get across the strait. No pleasure in picking up logs kicked out by choppy seas and wind."

A crow perched on the bow.

"What the hell?" Trig called out.

Darrell set his coffee down, got up and strained forward to see beyond the wheel.

"It's a bloody crow!" the skip said. "What's it doing this far out at night?"

Darrell noticed that Trig was worried. "Anything wrong?" he asked.

"No," the tug skip mumbled. He was lost in witnessing the bird perched on the bow.

The crow was oblivious to the cabin and its occupants. As the bow dipped, it spread its wings.

"He's away."

The crow flew back along the starboard side, caught the wind, turned and skimmed above the water on the port side and again alighted on the bow.

"Damn strange!"

Trig replied in a subdued voice, "It's one of those who've been singled out."

The crow cawed, rose, and swept again around the starboard and port sides. This time, however, it chose not to land. Instead, the bird flew once again around the *Stormer*, then winged back in the night sky towards land.

The tug was at full throttle and making a steady nine knots. "We'll soon meet up with the *Harmac Cedar*," Trig estimated while passing the beacon at Gabriola's southern tip.

Night was complete; the search beam split the dark, illuminating a three-string boom. The skip cut power, gripped the hand mike, and made radio contact with the tug they were to assist. "Where do you want us to hook in – up front alongside you, or…?"

"Can you get behind the string of log bundles and tie up to the adjacent flat raft?" crackled a voice shielded by static.

Trig turned the beam and observed the suggested position. "Can do." He maneuvered the *Stormer* behind the log bundle and beside the flat raft. Without a word, he turned the wheel handle on a watertight door, exited, and walked sternwards. With a hop, he was standing on a boomstick; with another leap, he was walking on the first raft from log to log. "Pass the line," he shouted as he returned over several waxy logs to grab for the rope.

The novice deck hand passed the line, and watched intently in the beam's light as Trig fastened the tow line to the boom chain. But on return, he couldn't hop on the boomstick alongside the tug. It had drifted out from the logs in the raft. He faced a watery gulf.

"Hand me the pike pole," he shouted.

When Darrell complied, Trig tried to hook the boomstick with the pole, but the stick was beyond his reach. "Damn," he muttered. "Turn the wheel one turn to port and let the tug push it back to me."

Darrell dashed into the cabin, turned the wheel, poked his head out the doorway to check if the plan was working. The craft turned to port, the bow pushed the boomstick back in, sealing the gulf. However, the stick came back too forcefully and nudged Trig's log. He shouted as he lost his balance, fell backwards, and slithered off a log, slipping below the water's surface.

Darrell numbed. There was only the sound of slapping water. He called out, "Are you there?"

No reply. Trig was under the logs.

"Oh hell," he shuddered. He swiveled the search beam scanning the log raft for his fallen partner. Dread knotted in his gut. "*Harmac Cedar, Stormer* here," Darrell stammered into the radio mouthpiece.

"*Stormer*, what's up?"

"The skip is under – no sign of him. Get a dinghy and search lights back here, fast."

"Check. Crew on the way. Get out on that boom and hunt."

Darrell didn't reply. He bounded out on deck and jumped on the log raft. He stepped precariously over the greasy logs. "Trig!" he yelled repeatedly. Only the sloshing sounds of waves answered.

A dinghy approached, lit with a lantern and carrying two men.

"Where'd he go under?" asked a hefty *Harmac Cedar* crew member.

"About two logs over."

"Water's frigid, April 'n all. He's been in near five minutes. If he ain't out of breath, exposure is settin' in."

"No time to fear the worst," said the other *Harmac* rescuer. "Spread out."

The men split apart, searching, probing for Trig Bjornson. Many logs were traversed, the searchers bent down at gaps and shone their lights into the water under the logs, half expecting to see a head or body pinned underneath.

"He's done sank," one crew member called.

Darrell's spirits sagged. 'Trig can't be gone. Too much savvy,' he thought.

Far off, near the marker lantern at the end of the boom, a parched groan. "He's back here!"

Forgetting the slippery logs, Darrell scrambled towards the voice. He spotted the skip sprawled over logs, legs trailing in the water. "God!" he cried, feeling queasy.

Trig must have come to and found himself immersed in the cold black sea, trapped under the logs with his lungs screaming for air, then lost consciousness.

One *Harmac* crew member held the light while Darrell and the other man lifted and rested the skip on the boom logs. One of Trig's arms was swollen and bloody, and a bone protruded.

"He's alive," Darrell uttered.

"Arm's a mess. We'll pack him back to the *Stormer.*"

The crew member holding the light called out, "Hey man – you hear that? There's a crow out here."

"Go to hell!" mocked the other man.

Darrell heard the flap of wings, and then saw the crow light on the raft.

He wished he had turned down the deck hand job and stayed with his buddies to get drunk.

Naked in the Mall

As I sipped my coffee in the Trail Bay Mall, I realized I was feeling the January chill more than usual. I quickly went through a mental checklist of the morning: shaved, brushed my teeth, showered, towel dried, put on my socks and shoes … but had I put on underwear, shirt or pants? Nope! I hadn't dressed.

'Just too preoccupied,' I thought.

I now knew why people had stared at me as I went through the sliding doors of the mall. I had thought that they were noticing my aura of self–assuredness, but it may have been my exposed jostling dangler that actually caught their eye. Or my pale cleaved buttocks.

The girl who served my coffee had looked at me sweetly, but with a slightly quizzical look and a light tinge of blush. "The cream is at the side," she nodded, trying to conceal her smile of disbelief as she looked in the other direction.

I sidled up beside another coffee patron stirring his brew with one of those elongated wooden medicine sticks. "Excuse me," I said as I reached for the whole milk canister.

He glanced over, sized me up, and with a disdainful sneer said, "Excuse you? Not likely."

Needless to say, I was offended, but in a perplexed way, since I had not yet clued in to my nakedness.

'Some people don't have the knack of being nice anymore,' I rationalized as I sat down at a table and reached for the latest edition of the *Coast Reporter*. I opened the newspaper and that's when I found it rather drafty in the interior mall coffee shop.

'Strange,' I mused. That was the very instant I became aware that I was revealing myself to the world.

'Oh God!' I swiveled on my chair while bringing my hands down to cover my pubic you-know-whats.

I was in a state of red-tilt panic. 'This is beyond dreadful.

How am I going to get out of here with any of my dignity remaining intact? Will I ever be allowed back into the Trail Bay Mall? Can I ever show my face in Sechelt again?'

I surveyed the coffee shop and the mall outside. There was a crowd beginning to form and I was the center of their attention. An elderly woman gagged on her Earl Grey at a nearby table; pensioners who often gathered for an afternoon coffee stopped talking and gawked at me in stupefied amazement.

Now, of course, there were toddlers scooped up by their horrified parents shielding their children from looking in my direction. But there was a little girl who caught a glimpse of me and exclaimed, "Mommy, why is that man naked?"

"Probably early dementia," replied the mom, recognizing that her daughter wouldn't understand the answer, but providing her with the time to quickly move in the direction of the end-of-mall grocery.

'Got to cover up,' I surmised, 'but with what?' I surveyed the table, reached for a napkin, unfolded it with trembling fingers, and slapped it over my exposed privates.

The counter girl was now engaged in a serious conversation on her cell phone and I quickly deducted that she had contacted mall security. A burly native man was running towards the coffee shop and I knew that he wasn't just in need of his daily caffeine fix.

"Hey, you! What gives?" he said in an angry voice as he approached. His chest was heaving as he struggled for breath; adrenaline was influencing his reaction to my audacity to sip coffee naked in the mall – his domain.

I shrugged. "Forgot to dress this morning." My face reddened and I could sense the stickiness of perspiration on my bum cheeks adhering to the leatherette chair.

"You'll have to go with me to the mall office where we can try and sort this out," he said. He peeled off his security jacket and extended his arm in a gesture for me to take his offering immediately. He grimaced, obviously upset, but somehow managing to act with some restraint, even tolerance. He appeared as a man who knew how to deal with a crisis situation, no matter how outlandish.

I wrapped myself in the jacket, felt warmer and less vulnerable through cloaking myself again, but sensed a diminished sense of freedom.

Nakedness allows the real me to be displayed, albeit with flabby imperfections, and not just in what I can afford to wear or what I want to express about the interior me through a choice of clothes. Dressing each day is like trying on different masks, creating an image or feel that is comfortable; allowing me to play with aspects of personality or daring to push the frontiers of who I am. I once accepted shirts from my brother who had a taste for plaids and stripes, but it wasn't me: I sensed that I had taken on some of his persona, aware of his presence and the memories associated with him. Similarly, wearing a faded denim jacket with frayed jeans in my younger days had made a statement of inner philosophy and my dissonant point of view of the world.

The security man grabbed my am, pulling me bare-legged towards his office. "What's with you man? What's with the no clothes? You got issues?"

"No, just absent-minded. A lot on my mind."

"You'll have lots more to think about soon. You're in a serious heap of trouble."

I passed an assembled crowd. Some averted their eyes; some gave me looks of disgust; others made rude comments, even obscene ones.

I hung my head in shame, although I felt that at least I was getting some recognition through my perverted infamy. Ahead of me I spotted Anthea, the head of a writing group I belong to, carrying a grocery bag. She was ambling towards me as the resolute security man tugged me along.

"Frank," she said with concern. "What's happening? Are you in some kind of trouble? Where are your pants?"

My head slumped even lower; I avoided eye contact with her. The guilt I felt was made even more palpable by meeting someone who recognized me.

"You know this person?" asked my captor.

"Yes, I do. He attends my weekly writing group."

"Does he … er … have any problems…?"

"Well … he isn't very computer savvy. Can't even attach an email."

"That's not exactly what I meant."

"Oh, I could add that he has a problem understanding metaphors. He takes things a little too literally, if you know what I mean?"

"Not really."

"Let me illustrate my point: he has difficulty accepting that a shadow could be like a drifting star – doesn't work for him."

"What I mean is, does he have more problems other than just being forgetful? Found him in the coffee shop naked as a newborn baby. Somewhat shocking, to say the least, for the senior afternoon shopping crowd."

"Not that I was aware of, but I must admit it does seem extremely odd."

How dreadful was my predicament. I remained mute, continuing to stare at the floor tiles. But then an idea sprang to mind … wouldn't it be interesting to have a Naked Shopping Day? The merchants could provide deep discounts for those willing to bare all. It might generate national interest even to the point of piquing international attention. Videos of the naked shoppers could be uploaded to You Tube. Sechelt, and even Trail Bay Mall, would become the focus of the world's attention as the videos went viral.

I paused in my train of thought as I realized just how many of those bargain-seeking shoppers would be well-advanced in age. The idea of all those aged, wrinkled and sagging bodies meandering from store to store was a bit too jarring.

The security man glanced back at Anthea as he continued to pull me towards the mall security office. "The authorities are going to deal with this guy."

'Authorities!?' I bloody well knew what that meant.

A shudder rumbled through my body and I looked around me. I was holding a coffee cup retaining a smidgeon of coffee and a few bits of suspended grounds at the bottom. And I had my clothes on!

"Would you like a refill?" the young counter girl asked me as she collected left-behind coffee cups.

"Huh? No – I think I've had enough."

So I wasn't naked after all, only lost in a fantasy that seemed all too real. I felt as though I'd wakened from a bad dream – the kind where you think for several minutes that the dream is reality and you go through all the thought processes and rationalizations of working out the dream content and its impact on your life. Perhaps you dreamed that you let a university semester go by without doing any of the required assignments, and that you are now facing the final exam; or that you attend a writers' group and haven't submitted any written pieces for the participants to critique; or that you are still in love with a long-forgotten girlfriend. Those scenarios that resurface from your seething subconscious to haunt your nocturnal present ... until slowly you accept that the dream was just that – only a dream.

But in my case, a daytime fantasy borne from the tedium of my coffee shop-hopping lifestyle had affected my sense of psychic equilibrium. I was now in the process of admitting I wanted more excitement in my life – perhaps someone to help change the mundane direction of my daily routines. Nakedness could be a life-changer, but the fallout from promenading around the Trail Bay Mall would be more than what I could cope with.

I spotted Anthea carrying her shopping in a recyclable bag. I guessed that seeing her had been assimilated into my day-dreaming.

"Hi Frank," she said: "Coming out Tuesday?"

"For sure," I replied.

"How's the writing coming along?"

"In bits and drabs," I answered.

"Good. See you then."

"Bye." I sipped on the last of my now-cold coffee.

'Why would I be ashamed if I was naked?' I mused. Where did the idea of shame come from? Was it just a cultural norm or did it have some religious roots?

Another attractive woman walked by my table. I felt a feeling of desire. 'Does that shame go back to Adam taking the apple-bite? He wasn't aware of his nakedness or that of Eve, his temptress. But suddenly, right after that first sin, he became lustful and had to cover up his growing attraction for Eve by hiding himself with a fig leaf.'

I pondered this further, still eyeing the woman who was now ordering a coffee. I noted the curve of her leg accented by her stretch pants and decided that clothes only add to the mystique. 'But they're just functional – just to keep us warm,' I told myself. I didn't completely believe it though … The imagination has a strong power to titillate.

The woman, now seated, became aware of me looking at her. She gave me a smug grimace. I averted my eyes, felt embarrassed, aware of my wanton feelings. My cheeks reddened to the colour of a pale apple.

I gathered up my newspaper, picked up my backpack and slung it over my shoulder, then left the coffee shop behind. I knew that the shop would now always carry reminiscences of idle nakedness.

12323735R00066

Made in the USA
Charleston, SC
27 April 2012